SILENT KILL

PETER CORRIS is known as the 'godfather' of Australian crime fiction through his Cliff Hardy detective stories. He has written in many other areas, including a co-authored autobiography of the late Professor Fred Hollows, a history of boxing in Australia, spy novels, historical novels and a collection of short stories about golf (see www.petercorris. net). In 2009, Peter Corris was awarded the Ned Kelly Award for Best Fiction by the Australian Crime Writers Association. He is married to writer Jean Bedford and has lived in Sydney for most of his life. They have three daughters and five grandsons.

Peter Corris's thirty-nine Cliff Hardy books include *The Empty Beach*, *Master's Mates*, *The Coast Road*, *Saving Billie*, *The Undertow*, *Appeal Denied*, *The Big Score*, *Open File*, *Deep Water*, *Torn Apart*, *Follow the Money*, *Comeback*, *The Dunbar Case* and *Silent Kill*.

PETER CORRIS

SILENT KILL

ALLEN&UNWIN
SYDNEY·MELBOURNE·AUCKLAND·LONDON

Thanks to Jean Bedford for advice and corrections.
Thanks to Jim Allen and Ben Smith for
geographical information.

First published in 2014

Copyright © Peter Corris 2014

Allen & Unwin
83 Alexander Street
Crows Nest NSW 2065
Australia
Phone: (61 2) 8425 0100
Email: info@allenandunwin.com
Web: www.allenandunwin.com

Cataloguing-in-Publication details are available
from the National Library of Australia
www.trove.nla.gov.au

ISBN 978 1 74331 637 5

Internal design by Emily O'Neill
Set in 12/17 pt Adobe Caslon by Midland Typesetters, Australia
Printed and bound in Australia by Griffin Press

10 9 8 7 6 5 4 3 2

For Tom and Linda

If there's any milk been spilt, I trust you to get it back
into the bottle ... Tidy him up.

—John le Carré, *Smiley's People*

part one

part one

1

Jack Buchanan walked into my office without knocking. He hadn't contacted me by phone or any other way and I hadn't seen him for ten years. But I knew him immediately— he was 190-plus centimetres and a hundred-plus kilos of unbridled energy. He shoved my desk aside as I got up from my chair behind it and threw a looping right-hand punch. Looping right-hand punches are easy to avoid if you know the drill. You can block with a forearm or duck. Ducking is best, because it leaves you set to put a hard short punch into an exposed ribcage. That's what I did and Jack staggered back, tripped over the client's chair and fell to the floor.

I stood over him the way Dempsey stood over Firpo.

'Go easy, mate,' he said. 'Just wanted to see if you still had it. Help me up.'

He stuck out his hand but I wasn't going to fall for that. When I took it I twisted hard so that if he wanted to come up he had to move the way I wanted him to. And he'd made a mistake. Jack, I remembered, was left-handed and that was the hand he'd raised. Should've raised the right and left his strong hand to do some work. He realised it as he came up and I kept the twist pressure on.

'Okay, Cliff, game over.'

I let him go and stepped back. Jack was an ex-commando, ex-stuntman and actor. We'd worked together on a couple of films and a TV mini-series, him as a stuntman and me as a bodyguard and armourer. If he'd been serious his next move would have been a kick to the balls. Instead he rubbed his wrist and elbow and bent to pick up the chair. It was old and heavy, not much use as a weapon. He righted it and sat down.

'I've got a job for you,' he said. 'Just wanted to be sure you were up to it. How old are you, Cliff?'

'Feeling younger every day. You've slowed up, Jack.'

'Tell me about it.'

'You mentioned a job. What kind of job?'

'Bodyguarding.'

'Who?'

'Rory O'Hara.'

'Jesus, are you serious?'

'You bet I am. I want you to look after Rory; he's one of my clients.'

'Clients?'

'That's right. We've lost touch. I run a speakers' agency

these days.' He looked around the room, which could best be described as functional. 'There's big money in it.'

It was late afternoon and time for a drink. It'd always be time for a drink for the sort of proposition Jack was making. I had a bottle of Dewar's in a drawer and ice cubes in the bar fridge. Paper cups. I made two drinks and handed one over while I prepared myself for Jack's pitch.

Rory O'Hara was a firebrand. He'd been a student agitator, a crusading journalist, had served a term in the Parliament of New South Wales as an independent and when he inherited a bundle of money, he became what he called 'a self-funded righter of society's wrongs'.

Jack took his drink. 'I know what you're thinking,' he said.

It wasn't hard to guess. O'Hara had blown the whistle on a massive development project in the western suburbs. The development had the backing of a fundamentalist Christian church, a major trade union, a superannuation fund and had attracted investment from a variety of sources including an outlaw bikie gang. The finances were shonky, approval had been secured through the corruption of local councillors and a state government minister, the environmental report had been falsified and the prospectus issued to attract investors had violated every regulation in the book. The plan had involved building a massive church, blocks of flats and an entertainment centre.

O'Hara had embedded people inside parts of the operation, accumulated evidence of all the misdeeds and published the results online. Vast amounts of money had been lost when the financial structure collapsed; several union officials, a fund manager, one of the local councillors and the state ex-minister were facing legal proceedings along with an auditing firm. It had been O'Hara's finest hour and soon after he'd been the victim of a hit and run. All this had scored the maximum amount of publicity. One thing O'Hara wasn't was publicity-shy.

I sipped my drink. 'So he's out of hospital, is he, after his accident?'

'If it was an accident.'

'Wasn't it?'

'Who knows? The man has enemies galore and he's nervous. Anyway, he's coming out the day after tomorrow.'

Jack reached into the breast pocket of his suit and produced a leaflet, which he passed to me. 'He's going on a big speaking tour. He'll attract very big, high-paying audiences. There's a documentary film being made and we've got a few high-profile TV interviews lined up. There's also a book deal.'

'More money,' I said.

'You bet. Take a look at the flyer.'

The glossy leaflet featured a photograph of a handsome, smiling O'Hara in a wheelchair. The message was simple: THERE IS MORE TO BE TOLD. THERE ARE MORE GUILTY PEOPLE TO BE NAMED. COME AND HEAR RORY TALK ABOUT HOW HE CLEANED UP ONE MESS AND PLANS TO CLEAR UP MORE.

There was a list of dates and venues for the weeks ahead—

several in Sydney, Wollongong and Newcastle and a dozen in regional centres along the coast and inland.

'Big itinerary,' I said. 'Is he for real?'

'He is. He's had people working for him for some time digging up the dirt. He's a genuine new broom.'

'I thought he was rich. Why is he turning himself into a money machine?'

'What he's doing costs a hell of a lot. It stretched his resources. He had to go to the US for one operation and you know what medical costs are like there.'

'I had a heart operation there. My fund covered it.'

'He says the health funds are essentially organised white-collar crime. He didn't have any cover.'

'Who hasn't he pissed off?'

'Nobody. You should see the hate mail—letters, emails, phone calls, death threats. The man has more enemies than . . . I can't think of anyone.'

'I suppose if he's that anxious you've organised some protection in the hospital.'

'Right.'

'Why not just switch it over to the tour? Can't see what more I could do.'

Jack finished his drink and leaned forward. 'Here's the thing. Rory's got an entourage—a personal assistant, a driver, a media adviser, several IT people handling the information he's accumulated—and there'll be a doctor and a nurse along. Some of these people have been with him for a while, some not. Also, he has a partner, Kelly Scott.'

'Male or female?'

'Female. Very. Do you get my drift?'

I nodded. 'I remember reading that O'Hara was hit coming out of his place in the late morning. So, if it wasn't an accident, someone knew his movements—where he was going to be and when.'

'That's it.'

'What did the cops do?'

'What would you expect? As little as possible. It could be that there's someone inside his organisation prepared to betray him. That's what he thinks.'

'What d'you think?'

'I think I can't afford to take any risks. This tour's going to be a circus and I've got a big investment in it. There'll be all sorts of possibilities to get at him. I want you to travel along with them and suss out the . . . traitor, if there is one, or at least give him some reassurance. You've got the experience. You can pick a wrong'un and you know how to deal with him . . . or her.'

'How would I join the circus?'

Jack shrugged. 'My representative on the tour, protecting my investment. As I say, I've put some money into it. I'm paying for the bus, subsidising the accommodation costs and the venue hiring.'

'What sort of money?'

'A lot, and I'm prepared to shell out to hire you. I'll pay your standard fee and expenses and there'll be a bonus at the end if it all works out well.'

'You're talking about a few weeks. That'll run up a bill.'

'I know. I'll sign a contract with you and pay you a solid retainer.'

'I'd have to drop everything else.'

Jack looked around the room again. He held up his empty paper cup. 'Dewar's is on special just now, I notice. You haven't had a phone call since I arrived and that clunky old computer isn't bleeping emails. I saw that crappy Falcon parked across the street. I don't get the feeling you're snowed under with work, Cliff.'

'I'd have to know more about O'Hara and a bit of time to think about it.'

'Google him. It's all there and pretty accurate. I've written the names of the people who'll be on the tour on the back of the flyer. My numbers are there, too, and my email address. I can give you until tomorrow.'

'How about you straighten my desk up?'

He grinned. 'Fuck you,' he said, and went out leaving the door open.

I went to the window and watched him exit the building. Long, confident strides. Maybe with a touch of bravado. He fished in his pocket for the remote and opened a silver Alfa Romeo parked illegally opposite. He had to ease himself into it; the fall he'd taken had hurt him more than he'd showed. He took off fast and showily. A big man with a big toy.

2

Jack had got me at exactly the right time. Business was slow and my live-apart lover, Marisha Henderson, had taken herself off to a high-profile job in Los Angeles. I wasn't altogether unhappy about that.

I'd driven her to the airport two days before. We'd been live-apart lovers for almost a year with the emphasis on the apart. There was an age gap and we had incompatible temperaments as we'd finally come to realise, and our compatibilities—sex, politics, tastes in music, senses of humour—didn't compensate. Marisha was ambitious, driven, ruthless even, while I'd seen too much to push and shove. I liked action, involvement, challenges, but I didn't expect rewards. Marisha did and demanded them.

The parting was going to be friendly and without tears. We'd make promises to visit, which we might or might not keep. She was looking splendid in black trousers and boots, leopard-print top and a black silk jacket. *Why are you letting her go?* I thought, but I knew the answer.

She touched my leg, setting up the tingle her touch usually did.

'What're you thinking, Cliff?' she said. 'Not missing me already?'

'That'll happen,' I said.

'What then?'

'Nothing.'

Marisha was one of those women, a minority I think, who dressed to be admired by men and I'd admired her and told her so often. She never tired of it and was probably looking for it now. Usually I would tell her how good she looked and mean it, but it didn't seem appropriate this time. She was put out. We went over a bump and the old springs in the Falcon announced their age.

'How many times have I told you to get rid of this piece of shit and lease something better?'

'Too often,' I said as I approached the ramp to the car park.

'Ooh, touchy.'

It was like that between us, snippy. Mostly we laughed about it but over time it had had an eroding effect. I found a parking space, unloaded her three bags, and we wheeled them past the machine where I'd later have to pay the fee that's said to be one of the highest in the world.

Marisha's high heels tapped on the floor as we went through the check-in procedures. Marisha wore high heels;

no comfortable travelling flatties for her. She had her visa and had been super efficient with her bookings on the web and encountered no difficulties with the baggage drop-off or anything else. We reached the international departures gate. Marisha had enough time to spare to have a drink in the VIP lounge and get everything in order—her newspaper, her iPhone, her Kindle. She hugged and kissed me without the usual care for her makeup.

'Stay in touch, Cliff. Often. I mean it.'

'I will. Knock 'em dead.'

'I will.'

A quick wave and she was gone.

I had missed her over the past days and I hadn't had enough work to keep me busy. Jack's proposition had its troublesome angles, the way a client's approach always does, but it promised activity and reward. Also, I knew Jack—he was an operator, but he played it straight, mostly. I unfolded the flyer and read the notes he'd written on the back. Eight names and functions were listed:

Penelope Milton-Smith, PA
Kelly Scott, partner
Clive Long, media liaison
Gordon Glassop, IT support
Sean Bright, ditto
Stan Tracey, driver

Dr Selim Chandry

Melanie Kim, nurse

I Googled Rory O'Hara. He'd been born in Bronte, only two suburbs away from Maroubra where I came from, but instead of a fibro house with working-class parents, he'd grown up with a rich father and socialite mother. Rory had a younger sister, an apartment in the city and a holiday home on the Gold Coast. He'd done arts/law at Sydney University and been president of the student council and editor of the university paper until ousted from both jobs by a right-wing coup as conservatives gained sway in the nineties. He'd won an election as an independent for an inner-city seat but resigned it after six months, declaring the parliament a useless oligarchy. He was thirty-eight years old, had been briefly married to a fellow student and had been a fitness fanatic and a low-handicap golfer before he'd been injured. His photographs shrieked silver spoon. Erect carriage, clear skin, perfect teeth.

I Googled the other names but only got results for Kelly Scott, Clive Long and Penelope Milton-Smith. Kelly had been a model and an actress who'd achieved moderate success at both without apparently trying very hard. In the photos she was gaunt, the way they are, and looked bored, but that may have been a professional pose. Putting dates on the two entries together, it looked as though O'Hara and Kelly had been an item for about eighteen months.

Clive Long had worked for the ABC, News Limited and

several commercial TV stations. He was the author of *Scratch My Back*, published on the web—an analysis of the interplay between politicians and the media. He was fleshy, with an angry tilt to his head. He'd been with the O'Hara bandwagon for two years.

Information on Penelope Milton-Smith was scanty but interesting. A swimmer, she had just missed out on selection for the Sydney Olympics. She'd qualified as a physiotherapist and then taken a degree in linguistics at Sydney University. Two photographs—one in a swimming cap and one with a mortarboard. Hard to assess her looks—handsome and healthy certainly. She'd been on O'Hara's skeleton staff during his brief parliamentary career after which she'd worked as a 'motivational speaker' before becoming O'Hara's PA fairly recently.

I thought about another drink and reckoned I could handle it if I had a meal to blot it up before I drove home. I sipped the drink and considered the job. You can't afford to be choosy with your clients and I'd taken on some I'd loved and some I'd hated. I was ambivalent about O'Hara. He was an attention seeker but he'd pulled the rug from under some people who thoroughly deserved it. He'd published all sorts of supposedly private documents and I had to wonder if this had made him vulnerable to legal action. That was a question to ask if I took the job on.

Don't kid yourself, Cliff, I thought as I worked on the drink. *Tripping up and down the coast in a tour bus like*

Kesey's Pranksters? Of course you're going to do it. But with eyes wide open.

There were interesting things to consider about the information I had. Why did Jack list the PA before the partner? Did that mean anything? And why the bus? Seemed an old-fashioned way of hopping about but I suppose flying that mob around would be expensive. The finances of the operation were a subject in themselves. Who would do the accounting?

I emailed Jack, attaching a contract and asking him to sign it and send it back. I also asked for copies of the death-threat emails and for him to make available copies of the threats that had come by other means. I ate Chinese with one glass of wine at a Pyrmont café and drove home sober.

Jack's email was there in the morning with the contract scanned and signed and the information I'd asked for. His thanks were brief. I printed out the material but before I had a chance to look at it the phone rang.

'Hardy.'

'Mr Hardy, this is Penelope Milton-Smith, Rory O'Hara's personal assistant. Rory would like to meet you. Are you free for lunch today?'

'I thought he wasn't getting out of hospital until tomorrow.'

'That's so, but he has special privileges in the hospital and we can arrange a catered lunch. Mr Buchanan said he'd engaged you.'

So Jack had got the wheels turning quickly. 'I'd be happy to come, Ms Smith. Just tell me where and when.'

'Thank you so much. The Greater Care rehabilitation hospital in Crows Nest at twelve-thirty. Parking is available.'

'I'll be there,' I said. 'Should I bring my gun?'

She laughed. 'I hardly think so, but if it makes you feel better.'

A win for her. No time to inspect the death-threat material and I thought it'd be better to meet the target first anyway.

The hospital was a converted Victorian mansion and, at a guess, an old building adjacent had been knocked down to make a car park. It was late April with a cool wind and I wore cords, a long-sleeved T-shirt and a denim jacket. I inquired for Mr O'Hara's room and was corrected.

'Mr O'Hara's suite is on the second floor,' the receptionist said. 'You'll have to give your name and show ID to the man posted there.'

'I should hope so,' I said.

The place didn't have a hospital smell because it was somewhere everyone came to get better, none to get worse and die. I went up the stairs to see if the guard was on his toes. These days, everyone expects the lift to be used. The door from the stairwell was just around the corner from where the guard sat. He had a clear view down a passage to the lifts but I was able to loom up beside him before he noticed.

'I took the stairs,' I said.

He jumped up and spun around. He was young, pudgy and trying to grow a moustache with limited success.

I opened my jacket, made a show of frisking myself, and showed him my driver's licence. 'Cliff Hardy. Expected and unarmed.'

He wore a rent-a-cop uniform with a pistol in a belt holster, a baton and a capsicum-spray shooter. His hands flew nervously from one weapon to another.

'Don't tell them,' he said.

'Tell them what?'

'That you snuck up on me.'

'Wouldn't dream of it.'

He pulled himself together and dialled a number on his mobile. I could hear it ring on the other side of the wall.

'Mr Hardy is here.'

The woman who opened the door stood 180 centimetres or more in her high heels. She wore a tailored charcoal trouser suit with a white shirt. She had golden blonde hair, olive-tinted skin and dark eyes. She wasn't beautiful but something more and better. She nodded thanks to the guard and gave him a wide smile. He blushed. She kept the smile going and gestured for me to go in. I caught a whiff of perfume as I went past her. It was there and then it wasn't, the way good perfume works, women had told me.

'Ms Smith,' I said.

'Milton-Smith.'

'With a hyphen.'

'Definitely. Rory's out on the balcony. This way.'

We walked through a sitting room with three doors leading off it. One was half open and I could see gym equipment. No mucking in at the hospital facility for Rory.

The balcony was glassed-in, capturing and holding the heat of the sun. O'Hara was sitting at a table. A walking stick rested in a fitting attached to the chair. He wore a shiny blue tracksuit with the top unzipped enough to show a silver neck chain on a tanned chest. He stuck out his left hand.

'Excuse me not getting up, and the left hand,' he said. 'Right shoulder's still a bit stiff from cracking it when I went down.'

The handshake was awkward.

I nodded. 'Shoulders are tricky.'

'You've had some injuries, I suppose?'

'A couple, but they patched me up okay. I gather you had complications.'

'Sit down. Yeah, fucking hospitals are infection traps. Jack Buchanan gives you a big rap. Can I call you Cliff?'

I sat. 'Sure, Rory.'

He laughed. 'Let's have a drink and some lunch. Pen, how about some wine and you shove some of this stuff on a plate. Christ knows what it is.'

There were two bottles of wine in an ice bucket and an assortment of dips and things on plates.

'It's vegetarian Lebanese, as you very well know,' she said.

She opened a bottle, poured three glasses, slid one across to O'Hara, another to me and took the third. 'To the tour,' she said.

We toasted. The wine was dry and cold which is all I ask of white wine. She busied herself putting things on a plate and adding dollops of dip. 'Help yourself, Mr Hardy.'

'Cliff,' I said.

She said, 'Pen,' and passed the plate with a napkin and a fork to O'Hara. I put a couple of pieces of falafel, a stuffed green pepper and some rice on a plate and spooned hummus over the lot. We ate and drank for a few minutes. The food was very good.

Pen had served herself generous helpings of everything and was tucking in. Siting relaxed with her jacket open she was shapely, with a swimmer's broad shoulders but lean. She drank the wine at more or less the same pace as Rory and me. Eating and drinking like that it was a sure bet she spent a lot of time running or in the gym.

O'Hara didn't eat much; he used his left hand mostly and found it difficult. A few times I sensed Pen wanting to help him but holding back. Eventually, he pushed his plate away and accepted a top-up of his glass.

'Jack says I've got a rat in the ranks,' he said. 'What d'you reckon?'

I forked in the last of the rice. 'Could be.'

'What would you recommend?'

I wiped my mouth with a napkin. Pen, who'd seemed to be mostly interested in topping up her wine glass, was suddenly engaged again.

'Sack 'em all,' I said, 'and hire a whole new bunch.'

He shook his head and I saw that the luxuriant dark locks were retreating a bit with an emerging widow's peak being screened by the hair falling forward. 'Can't do that. Those people have given up a lot to be with me. Jobs, partners . . . as far as I know everyone is loyal and committed.'

'As far as you know,' Pen said.

O'Hara thumped the table with his right fist and winced. 'Don't start! Sorry, Cliff. I'm very glad to have you along and I'll be grateful—for advice and insights.'

'And protection,' Pen said.

O'Hara nodded and suddenly looked tired. He put his hand on the walking stick. Time to go. I thanked him for the lunch, told him I'd see him on the bus. Pen took a large manila enevelope from her briefcase and walked me through the sitting room to the door.

'He's not strong enough,' she said. 'He shouldn't be doing this now.'

'If there's really someone out to kill him maybe he shouldn't be doing it at all.'

She stopped in her tracks. 'Do you doubt it?' She handed me the envelope. 'Copies of the death threats and transcripts of the phone calls.'

We were standing very close. I had a couple of glasses of

wine inside me and I could smell the perfume again. I wanted to touch her, had an urge to see if she was real inside that perfect shell. I stepped back. 'Running down's not killing, Pen,' I said. 'My job is to doubt everything and everybody.'

3

I drove home in a cheerful mood. Despite doubts about his sincerity and his long-term goals, and with an inbuilt distrust of the wealthy, I liked O'Hara well enough to find the job worthwhile. I'd liked Penelope Milton-Smith, too. Who wouldn't? She was efficient and warm. I wondered about her relationship with O'Hara. She was protective and perhaps more than that. She also had something on her mind.

I went home to collect the documents I'd printed out earlier, drove to the office and opened a hard copy and a digital file on the case. The five emails were from disposable gmail and Yahoo addresses, no doubt sent from public internet services. They were blunt, best summarised as 'Stop what you're doing or you'll be stopped'.

The four letters were computer-printed, literate and more explicit. They told O'Hara he was a menace to society—'a disruptive force' was one of the expressions used—and recommended that he devote his resources to worthy causes such as indigenous disadvantage. Like the emails, they appeared to come from the same or very similar minds, going by the language. The letters threatened in an oblique way, suggesting that O'Hara might want to think again before making himself a martyr in the interests of anarchic groups like the Occupy movement.

The phone transcripts were more varied and colourful. Jack's notes indicated that three of them were from male voices and three female. The female voices made disparaging remarks about O'Hara's sexual capacity while threatening emasculation, which seemed a bit contradictory, and the male ones hinted at information about him that was known and would be made public if he didn't cease his activities.

I read through them several times and then rang Buchanan. An underling put me straight through to him.

'What did you think of him?' he asked before I could speak.

'He's okay,' I said.

'And Pen?'

'You'd want her on your team.'

'Wouldn't you just. What's on your mind, Cliff? Bit busy right now. I've deposited the retainer in your bank.'

'Thanks. All that stuff came before the hit and run, right?'

'Right.'

'Nothing since?'

'No.'

'What do you make of those remarks to do with damaging information about him?'

'Bullshit.'

'No skeletons?'

'Your job's to protect, not investigate him. The bus leaves the hospital at nine sharp tomorrow. Pack a bag, and keep your receipts.'

I cleaned up the few unfinished bits of business in the office and drove home, where I washed and dried some clothes, left a note asking my obliging neighbour to collect my mail and made sure my laptop was fully charged and that I had all the connections to keep it running. I cleaned and oiled my .38 Smith & Wesson and packed it into a bag containing a selection of clothes I was likely to need from the south to the north coast and inland. I threw in Thomas Dormandy's book on the history of opium.

I rang my daughter Megan and told her I was off on a job for a few weeks. She knew that business had been slack lately.

'That's good,' she said. 'You sound up.'

'*On the road again,*' I sang.

'Okay, Willie, have a word with your grandson.'

Young Ben came on the line. 'Mum says you're off on a job.'

'That's right.'

'What sort of job?'

'Bodyguarding.'

'What's that?'

'Ask your mum.'

'Will you bring me back something?'

'What would you like?'

'A dog.'

Megan on the line: 'Don't you dare.'

'A boy needs a dog.'

'Yeah, and a dog needs a back yard, which we ain't got yet. Take care of yourself, Cliff.'

In the morning I caught a taxi to Crows Nest and saw the bus pulled up in front of the hospital. A group of people waited to get on. I hung back to look them over. I could pick the driver easily enough; he was getting in and out of the bus and opening two luggage lockers along the side. The dark-skinned man in the suit and the Asian woman standing next to him were obviously Dr Chandry and the nurse.

Of the other three men, one was fat and smoking furiously—the media guy, Clive Long, who'd put on weight since the web photo was taken. The other two were younger; both had laptop bags at their feet. One, the older and bigger, bulky in a leather bomber jacket, was stabbing expertly at his mobile while looking at the nurse. The other man, in a duffel coat missing a toggle, was flicking through images on an iPod—IT types for sure.

The morning was cold and I was glad of my leather jacket. The bus was sure to have air-conditioning, which would be welcome. As I approached, the group suddenly stopped milling about and took some shape.

Penelope Milton-Smith came down the path from the hospital. She was wearing jeans, boots and a Sydney University sweater with a big, thick scarf. She carried her briefcase in one hand and had a stack of newspapers under her arm. She nodded to the others and lifted the briefcase in a greeting to me.

'Hi, Cliff.'

'Morning, Pen.'

'Rory'll be here in a minute but we'd better get settled. I'll introduce you. What d'you want me to say?'

'Have you told them anything about me?'

'No.'

I thought about it. Bodyguard struck the wrong note, consultant was too vague. 'Just say security adviser.'

She went through the names as the people boarded the bus. All were polite, a couple were curious. Clive Long took a last drag, dropped his cigarette and stamped on it. He brushed ash from the front of his overcoat. His handshake was aggressive.

'I've heard of you, Hardy. Are we expecting trouble?'

'I hope not.'

'Then you'll just be along for the ride.'

'Hop up, Clive,' Pen said. 'Rory's coming.'

Long saluted ironically and hoisted himself up into the bus. I heard rhythmic tapping and turned to see Rory O'Hara, using an elbow crutch, coming down the path accompanied by a woman.

O'Hara was of medium height—say, 180 centimetres at most—and the woman topped him by a fair bit in only medium heels. Kelly Scott had filled out since her modelling days and it suited her. Under a faux fur jacket she wore a dark, long-sleeved dress in a soft material that seemed to flow over her generous figure as she moved. It had a high collar that accentuated her long slender neck. Her shoulder-length hair was a glossy dark brown and her features were strong. The catwalk boredom was gone; she exuded vitality as she gave O'Hara light support, just barely touching his free elbow.

'Gidday, Cliff,' O'Hara said. 'Kelly, this is Cliff Hardy.'

She gave me a nod and a smile that suggested she'd reserve judgement before deigning to speak to me. Pen had turned away and was talking to the driver.

'Ready to rock and roll, Stan?' O'Hara said.

Tracey gave him a thumbs-up, cleared his throat and climbed stiffly into the driver's seat.

O'Hara leaned against the bus and waved his crutch. 'Let's go then. I've been practising steps in the gym. I reckon I can get aboard all right. After you, Pen, Cliff.'

We went up the two fairly shallow steps and I looked back to see O'Hara following, placing his crutch carefully to help his left leg take his weight with Kelly hovering behind him.

The Volvo bus wasn't much smaller than a standard public bus, which made plenty of room for ten people and left space at the back for a toilet, a miniature office and kitchen and a bed. The seating just seemed to happen naturally, with the doctor and nurse beside each other, the two IT guys together already opening their laptops, Rory and Kelly at the back, Long on his own tearing open a packet of Nicorettes and me with Pen in about the middle.

Pen opened her briefcase and extracted some sheets of paper held together by a bulldog clip.

'Itinerary,' she said, detaching the top sheet and handing it to me. 'Maybe you should look it over first to see if you approve.'

'Is that you being ironic?'

She sighed. 'I don't know what I'm being. I don't know what we're doing here. It all seems wrong to me.'

'Getting the word out.'

'There are better ways.'

I looked the sheet over: it conformed pretty much to the outline Jack had given me, with the first appearance at the convention centre in Wollongong, followed by two in Sydney and a succession in Newcastle and north-coast centres and then a sweep through the inland from Armidale down to Goulburn.

'Why start in the Gong?' I asked.

She shrugged. 'A try-out, Kelly's idea. Sort of off-Broadway.'

'You know what my brief is, don't you?'

She grinned. She wore less makeup than before and I saw faint lines appear in her cheeks. They didn't make her less attractive. 'To stop a bullet, like Clint Eastwood.'

'No, to see if one of these people set Rory up for the hit and run.'

She'd been rummaging in the briefcase, now she turned towards me with her full attention. 'Whose idea was that?'

'Jack's.'

'Fucking Jack,' she said.

Now she had my attention. 'Better tell me what you mean.'

But she didn't respond. 'Shouldn't you be keeping it in the dark, what you're doing? Wouldn't I be a suspect?'

'Yeah, everybody is, but I'll stick out like a sore thumb anyway. I'll tell Clive next. He's dying to know and he'll tell everybody unless I miss my guess.'

She laughed. 'You're right there. Clive considers something a secret if fewer than a hundred people know about it.'

'What about Jack?'

She stared out the window and didn't answer. The traffic was heavy the way it is everywhere in Sydney these days and pretty well at all times. It was stop/start through the Harbour Tunnel and slow progress through Redfern. I waited for her to stop thinking and start talking but it took a while. The bus got into a long queue at the lights waiting to turn onto the Princes Highway. Probably not at this lights cycle, maybe the next.

'If you're thinking suspects,' Pen said at last, 'you should put Jack Buchanan at the top of your list, or near the top.'

'How so? He's got a big investment in this tour. Paid for it mostly, he said.'

'He said.'

'Not true?'

'I don't know. He's supposed to have sent me the breakdown of the figures but it hasn't come through yet. I'll be pressing for it as we go.'

'Still . . .'

'Buchanan's big investment is in the film and the book and the international interest in both. He's got the rights sewn up. Rory's supposed to be going to reveal stuff about a big political shake-up.'

'I haven't heard that before. What sort of stuff?'

'Wait and see. But I'll tell you this—at a certain point in this tour, at the end, say, Jack Buchanan stands to make more from Rory dead, as a kind of martyr, than alive.'

'I don't think Jack's that subtle.'

'Suit yourself. I shouldn't have said anything. You have a way of making people want to talk. How do you do it?'

'No idea,' I said, and I didn't even know if it was true.

4

As the bus picked up speed on the highway I heard movement behind me. Kelly was using a video camera to film the office where Rory sat at a desk with his crutch beside him. The chair was bolted to the floor and he had a seatbelt fastened.

'Kelly's doing the filming?' I asked Pen.

'Among other things.'

'Bit amateurish for a movie, surely?'

'Oh, she's an expert, apparently. But Jack's arranged for proper film crews at the venues. Kelly's stuff is just for hand-held authenticity.'

The bus was heated and most of the people had removed their coats and jackets, including Kelly. She moved sinuously down the centre of the bus, filming to either side.

'She's got a problem,' Pen said.

'What's that?'

'How to get herself in shot. Her natural film genre is film *moi*.'

I moved across to the seat next to Clive Long. 'What's your role in this show, Clive?'

'What's yours?'

I told him what I'd told Pen.

'Rules me out. I'm on the skids, alcoholic, prostate problems, emphysema. I need this gig to last as long as possible. I can't even tweet and twitter. That's why Bright's along.'

'Any ideas about who might think differently?'

'*Cherchez la femme*.'

'You mean the nurse?'

He laughed. 'You know who I mean.'

'Which one?'

'Take your pick. Scott's a gold-digger if ever I saw one. Out for herself a hundred per cent. In a way she's a bit like me, sort of washed up but scrubbing up better. God, did I say that? She'll play it to her own advantage all the way.'

'What about Pen?'

He shrugged. 'Don't know much about her although she's been around a bit longer than me. Sharp tongue at times. Who knows what her agenda is? Hates Scott, that's for sure. Probably has the hots for Rory, but I dunno. There's something about her. Seems too good to be true. Might pay you to . . . look into her, if you know what I mean. You seem to be well on the way in that regard.'

He hadn't answered my question about his job but I let it ride. I moved up to where Dr Chandry and the nurse were sitting and asked the doctor if I could speak to him for a moment. He was working on a laptop, which he closed before I could see what was on the screen. There were two vacant seats opposite. I slid across and the doctor joined me. Nurse Kim was doing something with her mobile phone. She looked up at me briefly. She was pretty but could have been much more so. Her dark hair was scraggly; she wore no makeup and her dress, under an unbecoming green cardigan, was drab.

This time I just said that I was there in a security capacity and I asked him about the state of O'Hara's health.

'It is not good.'

'What were his injuries, precisely?'

'He suffered a broken leg and pelvis.'

'But he's recovering?'

'Slowly. There was infection following the surgery, which set him back. He reacted badly to the antibiotics. He has had a very difficult time. He was immobilised for some weeks and the muscles have atrophied. He requires extensive physiotherapy.'

'Which he's not getting.'

'Regrettably, no.'

'What medications is he on?'

'I am not at liberty to tell you that.'

'Can you tell me who engaged your services?'

He hesitated. Unlike others on the bus, who'd shed layers, he was still wearing his suit coat over a sweater. Beads of sweat had broken out at his hairline. 'Mr Buchanan . . . it is not always easy to . . . yes, Mr Buchanan. He has been kind.'

He shot an anxious look at the nurse. He didn't seem like a candidate for anything, except writing prescriptions and telling people what they wanted to hear.

By late morning we were in Wollongong and booked into a city hotel where O'Hara was scheduled to give a press conference in the afternoon. Our rooms were all on the same floor with O'Hara and Kelly sharing. The two IT guys and, interestingly, the doctor and the nurse also shared double rooms, with Pen, Long and me in singles. Tracey apparently had family in the town and was staying with them.

I dropped in on Sean Bright and Gordon Glassop, the IT guys, gave them a vague account of my role and asked them what they were doing. Neither seemed very interested. Glassop was a weedy type in his late twenties, a bit stooped from hours at a desk and with a lip-licking habit. Bright was older and physically more imposing. He barely glanced at me, but I had an impression of clean-cut, slightly fleshy features and a full head of mid-brown hair. Both men were working at their laptops and were annoyed at having been interrupted. I noticed that Bright used his left hand to move the cursor.

'I'm checking Rory's speech for tonight,' Glassop said.

They'd ordered room service and had steak sandwiches and soft drinks at hand. Bright ignored my question until I asked it again.

'Research,' he said.

'Into?'

'Everything.'

I left them to it and found Pen and Long talking in the hallway. I listened.

'I've got two radio stations and the local rag coming to the conference,' Long said. 'A freelance who blogs prolifically, the local Greens candidate for the next election and someone from Get Up. Working on the TV. We're competing with a few local stories.'

'Like what?' Pen said.

'Drive-by shooting and a footballer's groin injury. I need something grabby.'

'Talk to Kelly. Knock softly. The doctor's given Rory a sedative but he mightn't be under yet.'

Long nodded and moved off towards O'Hara's room. Melanie Kim poked her head out of the room she shared with Chandry and looked up and down the corridor before ducking back inside. Just for a moment she seemed more animated and purposeful in her movements than I'd seen her before. Suspicious to the max, I wondered if she and the doctor were sharing substances as well as the room.

'Lunch?' I said to Pen.

She glanced at her watch and ticked something off on the top sheet on her clipboard. 'Why not?'

We ate at a café in the mall—fish, chips, salad and white wine by the glass. I asked her why Chandry seemed nervous.

She took a solid belt of her second glass. 'Have you decided to trust me, Cliff?'

I hadn't, but I liked her and wanted to. 'Provisionally,' I said.

She laughed. 'Good answer, must try to keep you guessing.'

With no sign of the appetite she'd displayed the day before—she'd only pushed her food around the plate and the wine had got to her—I wondered if she might've started drinking earlier. The rooms had mini-bars. 'He's very newly qualified to work in Australia. He doesn't want to make a mistake. Buchanan's said he'll help him establish a practice if he keeps Rory up to the mark.'

'He says O'Hara's not too good.'

'He would say that, wouldn't he? Has to look indispensable. Oops!'

She'd almost knocked her glass over, reaching for it. I pretended not to notice.

'I think I'm in love with him,' she said.

It wasn't what you wanted to hear from someone you were attracted to. 'The doctor?' I said.

She laughed loudly and kept on laughing quietly. She reached across and put her hand on mine. 'I'm glad you're along. You're a breath of fresh air.'

'That's me,' I said. 'You reckoned Jack has a motive to see O'Hara as a martyr. The doctor or the nurse could kill him. Clive could pinpoint his movements. Help them out.'

'So could I.'

'How about Bright and Glassop?'

She shook her head. 'They live in a different world, especially Gordon.'

'Is Bright like that, too? He looks more . . .'

'Only recently on board. Seems to know his job. He turns the charm on and off. Real live people don't mean anything to them.'

'That leaves Kelly.'

She drained her glass and got up unsteadily. 'I'm a bit pissed. Have to get back for some coffee and a sleep. Watch her, Cliff. Kelly'll come on to you if she thinks she should.'

I gave a waiter my credit card and we moved to the counter, then to the door.

'You haven't said much about Rory, Cliff. You think he could be a cipher, don't you?'

That wasn't my only impression. It was one of the things I'd thought about him but I knew that could be class prejudice. I had other more positive thoughts and I admired the way she'd picked up my uncertainty in our brief acquaintance. 'Too soon to tell.'

'Just wait till this afternoon and tonight. He'll light up the place. I don't want him to say what he's going to say but he will.'

'I don't follow. Is that why you're so jumpy?'

'Me, jumpy? That can't be right. I'm Ms Cool.'

5

Pen was right about O'Hara's impact. Leaning heavily on his stick, in a smart suit and open-necked tailored shirt, he was brilliant in the press conference. He handled every question thrown at him, was charming in answering the friendly ones and forceful with those less friendly. The event was held in a sort of meeting room in the hotel and I arrived early and took a very close look at everyone who came in. Clive Long was visibly nervous until a crew from the local TV station turned up. His job done, he went out for a smoke.

I wondered what they'd come up with to convince the TV crew to attend and it became clear near the end of the conference. In his answer to one question O'Hara revealed that he was forming a new political party to operate at the federal level. The big news was that he claimed to have pledges from members of all four existing major parties, Labor, Liberal, National and Greens, to defect to his party when it was up and running. With federal politics constantly in a knife-edge balancing act, that was enough to set rumour mills churning and journalists and bloggers tapping. O'Hara refused to name the potential defectors.

Pen had dressed up for the conference. In a white suit with a short, tight skirt and high heels, she orchestrated things skilfully, nominating the questioners and cutting the long-winded ones off. No sign of her earlier unsteadiness.

Kelly wore what she'd had on in the bus. She sat behind O'Hara and to one side, handed him water when he needed it and took charge of his crutch. Supportive, dignified, but overshadowed by Pen's sheen and control.

I caught up with Long outside the room as the meeting broke up and the mob dispersed.

'Disappointed in you, Hardy. You never once fingered an earpiece to show you were connected with SWAT team snipers.'

'Is that fair dinkum, about the new party?'

He shrugged. 'First I heard of it, but it set the bees buzzing. Made my job easier. How're you getting along with the hyphen? Shit, I almost said hymen, but I doubt that applies.'

I ignored the quip. 'What's it cost to attend the bash tonight?'

'Sixty bucks, but don't worry, you're—'

He was annoying me and I cut him off. 'How many expected?'

'Around eight thousand.'

SILENT KILL

'That's a fair chunk of money.'

He shrugged. 'Venue hire's high, insurance, ushers, band.'

'Band?'

'It's a show, Hardy. It's all a show. No more questions, please, I have to get outside for a smoke.'

I took a long walk around the city, testing my wind and legs on the hills. The place had a reasonably prosperous air, the way bay and seaside cities can, whatever the underlying problems. I went back to my room, drank instant coffee and kept away from the mini-bar. There was an email from Marisha telling me that she'd settled into an apartment and that the job was 'cool'. She asked me what I was doing and I gave her an outline. One of O'Hara's protests was at the stationing of American marines in the north and I asked her if that matter had attracted any attention in the US. She had signed off with love and I did the same.

O'Hara showed up well on the local six o'clock TV news. He looked damaged but vibrant and very appealing. Pen almost stole the show. The camera loved her and the small movements and gestures she made had that quality possessed by great actors—apparently unimportant but deeply significant by suggestion. The footage had been well edited and the new party bombshell went off just right.

The news was followed by a brief advertisement for the evening appearance with the information that a few tickets

43

were still available. The conference had achieved exactly what it set out to do—having seen it, or having heard people talk about it, you'd want more.

There was a knock at my door. I opened it to find Pen looking worried.

'What's wrong?' I said.

'Kelly's sick. She can't go to the meeting. She's staying back with the nurse. Cliff, take Dr C. with you and stick close to Rory.'

'Okay. What's wrong with her?'

'Don't know. I have to rush. Glassop and I have to supervise the set-up. Clive—'

'Clive what?' Long had appeared in the corridor.

'You'll have to explain Kelly's non-appearance to the media.'

'They'll be disappointed. I imagine she was intending to look her very best.' Long leered at her. 'But I expect you can do likewise if you try.'

Pen was wearing an eye-catching red suit. She ignored Long's remark and stormed off.

'Easy enough to take a gun into the convention centre,' Long said. 'Sit in the front row and . . . pow!'

'Hard to get away, though.'

'You think of everything.'

He drifted off and joined a group of four or five men and women who were waiting outside his door. I went to the doctor's room. He let me in and wiped sweat from his forehead. 'Most unfortunate,' he said.

'What's wrong with Kelly?'

He shrugged. 'I don't know. Perhaps food poisoning.'

'How's Rory?'

'Mr O'Hara is most upset. I've given him something to relax him.'

'I hope he won't be too relaxed. He has to perform.'

'No, no. He will be fine.'

We went into O'Hara's suite without knocking. O'Hara came from the bedroom, closing the door quietly behind him. 'She's asleep.'

'That is best,' Chandry said. 'Nurse Kim will stay with her.'

O'Hara had scaled back to a walking stick. He was wearing a perfectly cut dark suit with a white shirt and no tie. He moved athletically, just slightly putting some of his weight on the stick. He grinned at me. 'You packing, Cliff?'

His laugh had an edge to it and I wondered what Chandry had dosed him with. It certainly seemed to have invigorated him physically.

'Let's go,' he said. 'Kelly can strut her stuff another night.'

Tracey was waiting for us in a BMW at the hotel entrance. I took the basic precaution of having O'Hara ride in the back with me while Chandry travelled up front. It was only a short run to the venue which overlooked the city's golf course with the bay just visible to the east. The car park was full and there were people milling around the entrance. Tracey drove around to the side of the building and used a remote control to open a grille gate. We went down into a car park, which held only a few vehicles.

I told the others to stay put while I looked the place over. Tracey backed and filled until he had the car turned around ready to drive out. He turned on the interior light and unfolded a newspaper. I gave them the all-clear and Chandry, O'Hara and I headed for the lift.

The auditorium was full with a buzzing crowd, youngish and oldish, mostly casually dressed, being kept happy by an MOR rock band. The lights dimmed and the drummer signed off with some neat brushwork. Pen and O'Hara moved onto the stage. The lights went up and she introduced him to rousing applause. Chandry and I hovered in the wings.

'Thank you,' O'Hara said. He put his walking stick cross-wise on the lectern. It stuck out at either end and made a perfect prop, not obtrusive but impossible to miss. O'Hara's voice was strong and resonant and he maintained a perfect distance from the microphone throughout the address, but varying his emphasis and volume like an expert.

By now I was familiar with his themes—corruption at the heart of governments local, state and federal and the need for a new kind of person to bring honesty back into public life and corporate management.

He cited examples, named names, told jokes and worked the audience up into enthusiastic responses like a master showman. He didn't say much about his projected political party. He danced around the matter of the names of the defectors from the established parties, saying he wasn't in a position to reveal them yet but promised he would in due course. He mentioned one major and much-admired and loved political figure, albeit a retired one, he'd had discussions with.

He invited questions and Pen, in her red suit, moving across the podium and pointing, nominated the questioners from the many hands raised. Two women and ten men got the call. The questions weren't quite Dorothy Dixers but close enough. They enabled O'Hara to expand on certain points and slip in another couple of barbed jokes.

I'd found his performance compelling, if short on substance as to how the changes he advocated might be brought about. But the question and answer session struck the first real false note: the five people Pen selected were those I'd seen with Long outside his door in the hotel. Set-ups.

6

O'Hara chatted to people after the talk, signed autographs and posed for photos. A camera crew had filmed the proceedings, including a moment when a heckler had stood and shouted something. He'd been pulled down by the people around him and O'Hara barely paused in his delivery.

O'Hara leaned heavily on his stick as we headed back down to the car park.

'Are you all right, sir?' Chandry asked.

'I'm fine. Just tired. How the hell did Jacobs . . .? Never mind. Let's just get back as quick as we can.'

It didn't seem like the right time to ask him about the staged questions, especially in front of the doctor. Tracey folded his newspaper as O'Hara opened the back door of the Beemer.

'Anyone coming and going down here?' I asked the driver.

'Not a thing.'

O'Hara allowed Tracey to help him into the car and he sagged back in the seat. The vitality that had sustained him through the address, and through his restricted but smooth movements on the stage, seemed to have left him.

Tracey deposited us at the hotel entrance and drove off.

'I have to talk to Pen,' O'Hara said. 'That bastard . . .'

He didn't finish the sentence as he limped to the lift. Pen was waiting for us on our floor. O'Hara brandished his stick angrily and almost lost his balance. I steadied him. Before he could speak Pen had ushered us into O'Hara's suite.

'We've got a problem,' she said. 'Kelly's missing.'

'Missing?' O'Hara said. 'What d'you mean, missing?'

'Missing. Not here. Gone. The nurse as well.'

'Miss Kim,' Chandry yelped.

'Fuck Miss Kim,' O'Hara roared. 'How could she be missing? She was sick.'

There was no sign of disturbance in the sitting room. I looked into the bedroom. The covers of the bed were turned back but, again, nothing seemed seriously out of place.

Pen handed O'Hara a sheet of paper. He glanced at it and let it drop. I caught it. The message in large block capitals read: DO NOTHING. YOU WILL BE CONTACTED.

Chandry read the words and reached for the nearest telephone. 'We must have the police.'

Pen bumped him aside. 'We have to talk about this. Cliff, this is your territory. What d'you think?'

Chandry was sweating heavily again. O'Hara had collapsed into a chair.

'We'll stay here and look around,' I said. 'Pen, see if Kelly's clothes and bits and pieces are still here. Then do the same for Melanie Kim.'

Chandry buried his head in his hands. After a few minutes Pen returned.

'Kelly's stuff's still here, minus a coat I've seen her wearing. The nurse's clothes are gone, along with her bag.'

Chandry raised his head and stared at me. His damp hair fell lankly across his forehead and sweat had wrinkled his neat collar.

'Doctor,' I said. 'You have some explaining to do.'

Chandry said that Melanie Kim wasn't a nurse, or at least he had no proof that she was. A lonely, shy, inexperienced man, he'd been picked up by her in a Bondi pub where he'd gone to seek company and comfort. They'd had sex and, although he didn't say so, I got the impression it was his first time, or close to it. She said she was a nurse and pleaded with him to allow her to accompany him on the exciting exercise Jack Buchanan had hired him for.

'I could not resist her,' he said.

'You didn't ask for her credentials?' Pen said.

'He'd seen her fucking credentials,' O'Hara said.

'Please,' Chandry moaned.

O'Hara lifted his stick and for a moment I thought he was about to hit the doctor and moved to stop him, but O'Hara turned away with a disgusted snort.

'You're fired,' he said.

I shook my head. 'No.'

O'Hara swung back towards me. 'What do you mean, no? This man's not a doctor's bum-wipe and he's brought along some fucking hooker who—'

Chandry straightened in his chair. 'I am a graduate—'

'Shut up,' Pen snapped. 'Cliff?'

I told them all to calm down. 'This has been planned.'

'Jack,' Pen said. 'Boosting publicity.'

'Could be he hired the doctor as someone he could manipulate and he could have steered Miss Kim into her slot.'

'But he also hired you,' O'Hara said.

'Right. Why? Because we're old acquaintances and he could see I needed the work. He thought I was on the skids and wouldn't give any trouble.'

'Fuck,' O'Hara said.

'That's not very helpful, Rory,' Pen said.

'I need a drink.' O'Hara abandoned his stick, walked to the mini-bar with only the slightest of limps, pulled out a couple of miniature bottles of vodka and a glass and poured both bottles into it.

'I would not advise—' Chandry said.

O'Hara silenced him with a wave of his glass that slopped

vodka onto the carpet. 'So did he arrange to kidnap Kelly for publicity or . . .?'

'Or what?' Pen said.

'To control me?'

'Does he need to?' I said.

O'Hara took a slug of his drink and pressed his hand to his head. 'I'm a chemical mess. I can't think straight.'

Pen took a bottle of wine from the fridge, poured a glass, took a mouthful and looked at me.

'So you don't think she's in danger?' she said.

'Kidnap's easy to fake. And it's not exactly a threatening message.'

O'Hara scowled at me. 'What're you saying?'

'Nothing, yet, but this smells very fishy to me. Melanie Kim couldn't abduct Kelly on her own even if she were sick. And Kelly wouldn't go without a struggle if Kim had help.'

'The nurse . . . Kim, could've drugged her,' O'Hara said.

'Even so. Sean Bright was here. Let's see if he has anything to say.'

O'Hara was halfway through his quadruple vodka, which seemed to have revived him. 'Get Clive, Pen. We have to keep this under wraps.'

Pen left. Chandry started to get up but O'Hara jabbed his stick at him. 'You stay put. You're in big trouble, *Doctor*.'

'Easy, Rory,' I said. 'I think the doctor's a victim here too.'

'Thank you,' Chandry said.

O'Hara backed off. 'You implied that Kelly went willingly. That there's no victims.'

'We're all victims,' I said. 'It's just a question of whom and what of.'

Pen returned with Long and Glassop in tow. She'd evidently briefed them.

'Sean's gone,' Glassop said. 'Bag and baggage, and he took my fucking laptop, the bastard.'

Long popped a Nicorette. 'You're the security guy, Hardy. What do we do?'

'Contact Jack,' I said.

O'Hara reached into his pocket for his mobile. 'I'll ring him.'

I shook my head. 'No. We go back to Sydney tomorrow as scheduled and we see him in person.'

'Who does?' Pen asked.

She'd left the wine bottle on the coffee table. I took a glass from where the tea and coffee makings sat and poured. 'We all do,' I said.

7

O'Hara mumbled something about a sleeping pill; Pen argued with him and shepherded everyone out. Long and Glassop went down to the hotel bar. Chandry refused their invitation and went to his room with his shoulders drooping. In my room I turned on the TV and watched a couple of news programs and a documentary without absorbing any of the information. It looked as though my hoped-for month of employment was only going to last one day. I had a lot of questions for Jack Buchanan and a few for O'Hara and Pen.

In the morning we found that Chandry had vanished. At reception Pen somehow smoothed over the fact that nine had checked in and only five were departing. Tracey rolled up in the bus. Pen didn't offer him any explanation and he didn't ask. Not his problem. Taking our seats, we were all acutely aware of the absentees.

I went back to where Pen and O'Hara were sitting in silence. The video camera Kelly had used was lying on a nearby seat as a mute reminder of everything that had gone wrong.

O'Hara was visibly hungover and aggressive. 'You should've kept an eye on that fucking doctor,' he said.

'Yeah, and you've got some questions to answer.'

Pen drew closer to O'Hara protectively. 'Like what?'

'Like why you had plants in the audience to ask the easy questions.'

O'Hara shrugged. 'Standard practice.'

'Okay, this is harder—who is Jacobs, what was his interjection about and how come you had people there to shut him up?'

Pen shot me an angry look. 'Tell him,' she said.

'I'm too worried to think,' O'Hara muttered.

Pen drew in a deep breath. She was back in her casual clothes but with her hair and makeup perfectly in place. Although red-eyed, O'Hara was shaved and neatly dressed. I'd noticed that his suit was properly arranged in its bag, something I doubted he'd do himself. Not hard to guess that they'd spent the night together.

'Harry Jacobs is opposed to everything Rory stands for,' Pen said. 'He's a spokesman for every reactionary cause in the book. You must have heard of him.'

'I don't pay much attention to people like that,' I said.

Pen seemed to need physical contact with O'Hara, as if she was insecure about the relationship. She moved fractionally still closer to him. 'You should, they're dangerous.'

O'Hara was one of those people who don't like being left out of the conversation. He rallied. 'Jacobs also used to be Jack's partner in the agency.'

'This is all news to me,' I said. I was cursing myself for not looking more closely at Jack's operation before signing on.

'Jack had the contacts to book MOR types and radicals like me,' O'Hara said. 'And Jacobs booked the shock jocks and Nazis. There's money both ways.'

'You said they used to be partners.'

'That's right. Jacobs pulled out when Jack took me on. A bridge too far.'

Pen was staring out of the window but I doubted that she was seeing anything. I asked her why she didn't want O'Hara to have mentioned Jacobs. O'Hara opened his mouth to answer but she stopped him with a hand on his arm that was now more possessive than protective.

'Jack doesn't want anyone to know about the state of his affairs.'

'Which is?'

'He's suing Jacobs and Jacobs is suing him. His finances are on a knife-edge.'

'He paid me a solid retainer.'

'Probably borrowed it,' O'Hara said. 'He's borrowed a fair bit from me. This tour was supposed to get us both back on our feet.'

'That looks like a washout now,' I said. 'Could this Jacobs have got to Kelly and Bright and the nurse?'

'It's possible,' Pen said. 'He has bags of charm. There's a rumour that he had an affair with Kelly back when she was acting. He was a backer for one of the pictures she was in.'

'Just a rumour,' O'Hara said.

Pen patted his arm. 'You put money into one too and look how you ended up. It's her style, Rory. Her middle name is exploitation.'

'Don't,' O'Hara said.

I left them. Glassop was busy with his iPhone. I sat beside him and waited until he'd finished whatever he was doing. He looked up at me nervously.

'How long have you known Sean Bright?' I asked.

'Don't know him at all. Only met him a couple of weeks ago.'

'I thought you were a team.'

He did his lip-licking thing. 'No. Me and another bloke had worked for Rory for a while but he had an accident just before this tour got underway. I met Sean at a seminar and we got along. He was a fill-in.'

'Was he good?'

'How d'you mean?'

I opened my hands. 'At IT and all that.'

'Are you any good at it, Mr Hardy?'

'Hopeless.'

He took a long time before answering, as if he didn't want

to make a judgement. Good at computers, maybe he wasn't much good at people. 'He was all right, I think.'

'That isn't much of an endorsement.'

'Like I said, I didn't know him that well. Do you mind if I get on with what I'm doing?'

It cost him a bit to be that forthright.

'Why would he steal your computer? Did you lose anything?'

'I don't get you.'

'Anything sensitive?'

'Anything sensitive I encrypt.'

'Like what?'

He licked his lips again and didn't answer.

'So, did you lose anything?'

He reached into his jacket pocket and took out a bunch of keys with a thumb drive attached. He gave me a look of contempt, then blinked nervously at his temerity. 'Anything important's all here.'

I went back to my seat to think things over. Duplicity comes with the territory, but the layers of it here were out of the ordinary—shaky finances, warring partners, old love affairs and a new alignment of the players. It was a lot to process.

Traffic thickened after the freeway and we slowed to a crawl with delays at every set of lights and intersection so that the morning was well advanced before we went over the bridge adjacent to Tom Ugly's. The Georges River was grey under a leaden sky.

Long dropped into the seat next to me. His breath, hair and clothes smelled of tobacco smoke and his eyes, slits crinkled by a million deep draws and exhalations, were cynical and amused.

'Anything I should know?' he said.

Why not? I thought. I told him what I'd just been told.

'Knew it was too good to be true,' he said. 'I was going to write the fucking book. You'll be out of a job, too.'

'I'll survive.'

'Harry Jacobs, eh? Maybe there's a book in all this after all.'

'Is he capable of orchestrating something like this?'

'Harry? Sure he is. Some people think he arranged the—'

A strangled yelp came from the back of the bus. Pen, clutching her phone, was struggling to release her seatbelt. She unbuckled and lurched forward, grabbing at the back of the nearest seat for support. O'Hara reached for her, dislodged his stick and swore as it clattered to the floor.

'What, Pen, what?' he almost screamed.

Pen, wild-eyed and trembling, was brandishing her phone. 'It's Kelly,' she said. 'She's with the police. She says Sean Bright has killed the nurse.'

8

That was the end of the Rory O'Hara tour and of his high-visibility radical campaign. The police interviewed all of us who'd been on the trip and they were less than happy about no one reporting the abduction of Kelly Scott.

I came in for some stick. 'You should've known better, Hardy,' one of the coppers said. 'But I suppose it's the sort of irresponsible behaviour we should expect from you.'

I said the thing looked staged to me and part of some non-life-threatening, off-stage power play between O'Hara and Buchanan that had somehow got out of control. The officer was unimpressed.

The newspapers and television made a meal of the kidnapped girlfriend, the Asian accomplice and the cock-up that ended in Melanie Kim's death and her killer's escape and disappearance. Kelly hadn't been able to tell the police much about what had happened. Kim had drugged her and she and Bright had driven to Sydney that night to a motel, where they'd argued about, she thought, drugs and money.

This came out in a paid interview she gave to a TV station. While still under the influence of drugs, she said she'd heard a scream, staggered out of the bathroom where she'd been sick and found Kim dead, with her throat cut and Bright gone. Doctors confirmed that she'd been given a heavy dose of two drugs and could not possibly have wielded a knife so efficiently. There was no blood on her or her clothing.

The police and journalists dug deep but found nothing on Bright. It appeared that the name was an alias and that the credentials he'd offered Jack and others were faked. His true identity was a mystery. It was assumed he'd arranged the accident to O'Hara's previous IT guy and established that he'd scraped an acquaintance with Glassop at an artificial intelligence seminar.

Melanie Kim was a prostitute whom Bright had steered into Chandry's path. Chandry had been hired by Jack Buchanan on the cheap. A photo of Bright lifted from Kelly's video was published in the papers and circulated. It was a bit blurry and I didn't think it was a very good likeness, but I hadn't paid him a lot of attention. For fear of libel and contempt charges, the reporters steered clear of the dispute between Jacobs and Buchanan, which was headed for court. The story played for not much more than a week until it ran short of oxygen and died.

'Not your finest hour, Cliff,' my old friend ex-deputy

commissioner of police Frank Parker said one night when we were having a drink.

'Nobody's,' I said. 'Jack Buchanan says he's broke. I did hear that O'Hara's split with Kelly Scott and taken up with his PA, but I've no idea what they're up to. Probably licking their wounds in Bellingen or somewhere. Clive Long's supposed to be doing a book about O'Hara and the whole thing, but he'd need an explanation and an ending.'

'You didn't spot the nurse or Bright as something other than what they seemed?'

I shook my head. 'I was lazy. I scarcely paid them any mind. Looking back there were probably signs but I was thinking Harry Jacobs could be the disrupter or maybe there was jealousy between the two women.'

'Well, one got what she wanted.'

'I think she wanted him in better condition. Tell you the truth, Frank, the whole thing pisses me off. What was Bright really doing? Had someone put him up to it and if so who? Did he just fuck it up, or what? It eats at me a bit.'

'I'm sure it does. I know how stubborn you are.'

'Yeah, but I can't afford to be stubborn about this. I've got overheads. I have to keep drumming up trade.'

He nodded sympathetically and we went on to talk about other things.

I'd mollified grandson Ben with a do-it-yourself dinosaur assembly kit, dinos being his current obsession. I kept busy with routine jobs. A few long overdue payments came in when some court cases were settled and I kept my head above water. I worked out at the Redgum gym. Played some pretty good pool at the Toxteth Hotel and spent a few weekends with an old girlfriend down on the Illawarra coast. A balanced life, I told myself, work and play, but my thoughts often returned to that moment on the Volvo bus when Penelope Milton-Smith's announcement meant things fell apart, leaving only questions.

The man who phoned me had a strong Korean accent but his English was perfectly grammatical. He said his name was Neville Kim, that he was Melanie Kim's brother and that he wanted to see me. He kept the appointment precisely on time and came into my modest office with the bearing of a man used to bigger and better things. I'm no judge of suits, but his looked expensive and his shirt, tie and shoes looked the same. He was big, at least as tall as my 190 centimetres, and broader and thicker. His handshake was firm and dry.

'My sister was a lost soul, Mr Hardy,' he said, 'but we loved her.'

I nodded.

'We in the family blame ourselves, in a way. Melanie was beautiful but . . . unfocused. Others of us have achieved a lot in this country and she felt . . . undervalued. Perhaps that's why . . .'

He trailed off uncertainly, which seemed to annoy him. He took a deep breath and his massive chest rose.

'The police, in my judgement, have been less than diligent.' He shrugged. 'An Asian prostitute involved with a criminal. Who can blame them? But I am not satisfied. I want the man Bright brought to justice and I want to understand what happened.'

'I can see why you would. I feel much the same for different reasons.'

It was his turn to nod. 'Professional reasons, yes. Your name was mentioned in several news stories and I took the liberty of making some inquiries about you. I'm satisfied that you are honest, discreet and capable. I want you to investigate the circumstances surrounding my sister's death.'

Neville Kim gave me his card. He said he had dual Korean and Australian citizenship and was the CEO of an electronics company I'd vaguely heard of. Its office was in a prestigious part of the CBD. He lived in Bellevue Hill. I informed him of my rates and charges and he smiled and asked if I preferred the retainer in cash, by cheque or direct deposit.

'You knew I'd accept the job,' I said.

'I was told it was likely you'd be dissatisfied with the way things had worked out.'

'Who told you that?'

He smiled again. 'A confidential source. I'm afraid I can't offer you any help at this point. My sister's life was laid bare in the media and the reporting was mostly accurate. I knew nothing about Bright or Rory O'Hara beyond what I learned after Melanie's death. The press quickly lost interest. Only one rather blurry photo of Bright was ever published. As far as I could tell from their interview with me, the police investigation was perfunctory. I have ... technicians at my disposal, should you need them.'

I was still kicking myself for not checking on Jack Buchanan before accepting his job. If I'd known he was locked in litigation with an ex-partner and his finances were dodgy I might not have played things differently, but at least I wouldn't have been surprised and a bit distracted when the information came my way.

I didn't make the same mistake this time. I researched Neville Kim as thoroughly as I could and he came up trumps. His company was prosperous and he was respected in the business community. The connection to Melanie had been made in the press but treated sensitively. Kim was a leading light in the Sydney Korean community, a family man with an attractive wife and three children. Time to get busy.

No private inquiry agent can survive and prosper without a police contact. After I recovered my licence it took the best part of two years before I was able to cultivate that sort of a relationship with a police officer. Detective-Sergeant Colin Williamson was based in Glebe but he'd participated in a number of highly successful police operations and was frequently co-opted to squads assigned to big-time cases. He'd been in on the capture of a notorious and violent criminal who'd escaped from gaol and he'd talked down a couple of siege-stagers—one threatening members of the public and one holding a policewoman hostage.

I'd met Williamson in the Toxteth. I'd played pool against him, had a few drinks, shared a pizza while watching boxing on TV in the pub and we'd become wary friends. I called him at the Glebe station and arranged to meet for a drink that evening.

Williamson was in his early thirties, youngish for his rank. He wasn't sure that he wanted to remain a policeman and was pursuing a part-time law degree in a desultory fashion. But his successes and his intention to marry the woman he'd rescued seemed likely to result in the police service being his life. His uncertainty made him more objective about his role than most cops. He knew I was a friend of Frank Parker and that being a friend of a friend of Parker's wouldn't do him any harm.

We took glasses of merlot and the pub's offering of biscuits and cheese cubes into a quiet section with comfortable seats. Williamson was medium tall, thin but wiry with a face slightly scarred by youthful acne. He was sensitive about it and often held a hand up protectively to his lower jaw on the right side. The gesture made him look thoughtful, which he usually was when he was with me.

'So, Cliff,' Williamson said, spearing a cheese cube with a toothpick. 'How's it going?'

'You know I've been doing these pissy little jobs for a while now. Just paying the bills, or nearly.'

'Isn't that what we all do?'

'Such cynicism in one so young,' I said. 'The thing is, Col, a bigger job has come my way and I'm going to need some help.'

He grinned, ate his cheese and crunched a biscuit. He held up his glass. 'Is this where you corrupt me with a glass of red and letting me win at pool?'

'I never let you win. I hate to lose as much as you do, maybe more. No, I need some information on an operational police matter, or you might say a non-operational matter.'

That hooked him, as I knew it would. I sketched in the O'Hara story, which he was already familiar with, and told him about the Neville Kim commission. He leaned back in his chair and took a decent pull on his glass.

'Shit, isn't that typical?' he said. 'Some poor Asian hooker . . .'

I shook my head. 'That's just the point, Col. She wasn't only some poor Asian hooker. Her brother said she was bright and felt undervalued. People like that often want to prove their worth. I think she was playing for higher stakes.'

9

Williamson looked sceptical. 'Why do you say that?'

'She downplayed herself in every way. Now that was obviously an act, though I didn't know it at the time. Then, just once, I caught a glimpse of her in a completely different mode.'

'As the hooker, you mean?'

'No, something else. Something . . . determined.'

'That's very thin, Cliff.'

'I know. It was just a feeling, but there's a vagueness to all this that worries me. The newspaper reports say Kelly Scott heard Bright and Kim arguing about drugs and money. That strikes me as glib, too easy. I'm wondering how hard your boys pressed her. They certainly didn't push me very hard.'

He sighed. 'Now we're getting to it.'

We'd both finished our drinks and I got up for more, firing one parting shot. 'How hard did they look for Chandry?'

I brought the drinks back and we ate some more of the cheese and biscuits, both thinking our thoughts.

'I'll ask around,' Williamson said.

I raised my glass. 'Thanks, Col.'

'Think there'll be anything in it for me?'

'You never know.'

'True. Have you got a theory?'

'A very shaky one. What if the hit and run was really just an accident and someone put Bright and Kim into the mix just to keep an eye on O'Hara and stop him if they had to?'

'Someone? I haven't followed this too closely. You're thinking of . . . ?'

'Harry Jacobs, or someone behind him.'

'Go on.'

'What if O'Hara's announcement about a new party and having people on board was a catalyst for Bright and Kim to grab Kelly Scott and apply the pressure?'

'Yeah. And it worked.'

'But what if Kim had another idea—get the names of the people and make a big splash. Think of the headlines.'

'So Bright kills her. Jesus, you're stretching it, mate.'

'It's just a theory, as I said.'

'Theories have to be tested. How're you going to do that?'

'By talking to Kelly Scott and seeing what you come up with.'

* * *

The following morning I phoned Jack Buchanan and asked him if he had a contact number for Kelly. He wasn't pleased to hear from me.

'Fuck you,' he said.

'Litigation not going too well?'

'I'm fucked.'

'Tell you what, Jack. I'll give you back the retainer you paid me.'

Despite himself he laughed. 'You cheeky bastard, but I'll take you up on that.'

'Okay, so ...'

'I heard that Kelly's back on the drugs.'

'Back on them?'

'You saw her. She's naturally a well-built chick. How d'you think she got the waif look when she was modelling? Wouldn't surprise me if she's on something pretty hard.'

'Do you know where she's living?'

'No, but one of my clients ... former clients, said she's doing some dress designing for a company in Surry Hills called Fringe Clothes. Bit of a sweatshop, she reckoned. I suppose she's trying to work her way back into modelling.'

I thanked him, then I repaid his retainer, which I'd done nothing to earn. It was no sacrifice because Neville Kim had given me a password, which gave me access to a bank account with a six figure balance. Fringe Clothes was in Riley Street, Surry Hills. I caught a taxi. I was working, charging Kim at my top daily rate and on expenses.

The place was a narrow two-storey terrace with a very small sign on the gate outside. I rang the bell and a woman answered the door. She was middle-aged, dumpy, wearing a wrinkled dress and a cardigan that had seen better days. I showed her my licence and told her I was looking for Kelly Scott.

'What's she done?'

'That's not your concern. Is she here?'

'No.'

'Can you tell me where she lives?'

'No.'

I could hear the sound of machines humming inside the house. I pushed past her and saw that the shabby ground floor of the house had been gutted to form a large open space. Ten women were working at sewing machines on benches. Most of them were Asian; a couple looked very young.

'You can't just barge in—'

I cut her off. 'One phone call to Fair Trading and you're in trouble. I very much doubt if this place is properly wired for factory work. Have to wonder about fire safety and the work permit status of some of these women.'

Several of the workers looked alarmed at my intrusion, but most just kept their heads down. A couple of the young women were pretty. I took out my mobile phone.

'Have to wonder,' I said, 'if sewing's all these women do.'

The woman threw a look at the stairs leading to the upper level.

'All right,' she said. 'I don't want any trouble. Kelly lives across the street in 23A. She came in asking for designing work and I'm giving her a try. What's wrong with that?'

I moved towards the door. 'I'd advise you to clean this place up. Check the ages of your employees. Put in a tea room, do something about getting an inside dunny.'

'How did you . . . ?'

'I know your type,' I said. 'Watch your step.'

I left, waited for the traffic and crossed the road. The sweatshop woman watched me, looking worried. There was a chance she'd put something right, just a chance.

Number 23A was a terrace of the same design as the one across the street, but it had had the treatment—repaired or replaced tiles on the porch, white-painted front facade with the window surrounds picked out in black. Solid window bars and an olive green door behind a security screen built to repel all boarders. I rang the bell and heard it sound melodically inside.

After another ring soft footsteps approached the door and I heard a body press against it to use the spyhole. Then the door opened.

'Jesus Christ,' Kelly said. 'Hardy. What're you doing here?'

'Hello, Kelly. I want a chat.'

It was strange to be aware that, after all the thinking and checking I'd done about her, these were virtually the first words we'd exchanged. She was wearing a thin, short silk robe with a Chinese pattern. She'd lost some weight but was a long way from the waif look, as Jack had described it, and neither weight loss nor the hectic brightness of her eyes suited her. She'd been putting on her makeup and still held a tube of something in her hand.

'What about? No, I don't want to talk to you. Go away.'

She fumbled when she tried to close the door; a lot of shapely breast was revealed as her robe fell open and she clutched at it.

'Let's not give the street a show,' I said.

It was simple to ease past her and let the door close behind me. She glared at me and dropped her hand so that the robe parted all the way and her breasts were completely uncovered. She wore black lace panties.

'There's a private show for you,' she said.

'Cover it up, I want a talk, not a fuck.'

'What's wrong with you?'

She was angry now, had straightened up and regained some of that arrogant superiority I'd seen in her before.

'Kelly, you're a beautiful woman and in another time and place I'd dodge heavy traffic to get to you, but now I'm working and I'm more interested in what's in here.' I tapped the side of her head with a finger.

She closed her robe and jerked her head at the stairs. 'Better come up to my room.'

'It's not your place?'

'Shit, no. I'm renting and sharing and she's in the kitchen. Come on up.'

The house had been thoroughly renovated with good lighting, carpet on the stairs and, unlike my place, no missing supports on the staircase bannister. Kelly went into one of the rooms off the landing at the top of the stairs. I followed her in and found her standing in the middle of the room naked.

'You sure?' she said. 'I like an older man and I quite liked the look of you back there before all this happened. What's your first name again?'

Her skin was a pale ivory shade; she was waxed smooth with her pubic hair shaven. She lifted her arms to her head and her firm breasts rose, the nipples firming. She'd have aroused the Pope.

'My name's Cliff. For Christ's sake put something on, Kelly. You don't like older men and you don't fancy me. You're playing games.'

She gave a sulky grin, picked up her robe from the floor and slid it on. She sat down in front of a dressing table with a large mirror and set about making up her face.

'Say what you have to say and be quick. I've got an audition.'

'Acting?'

'You bet acting. This time I'm going to fuck my way to the top.'

'What about dress-designing?'

'So that's how you found me. I'll dob in that bitch across the street.'

'Good luck,' I said, and surprised myself by meaning

it. 'D'you remember being interviewed by the cops after Bright shot the nurse?'

She used a brush on her smooth forehead. 'Sort of.'

'I think you were lying when you said you heard them arguing about drugs and money.'

The hand moving the brush paused for just an instant before resuming its work.

'You do, eh?'

'Yes. I think you heard them arguing about something else.'

She spun around on the stool and looked at me. 'Go on.'

'What was it?'

'What do you think?'

That wasn't the way to play it; the idea was to draw her out but she'd taken the initiative.

'I was right,' she said. 'People think that a woman who looks like me has no brains, but they're wrong. I had a feeling someone'd ask me this question some time.'

'What's the answer?'

She hurried through the makeup process. She put on the panties she'd dropped to the floor, walked to the closet, selected tights, a shirt and loose pants and dressed. She got a pair of stilettos and slid into them.

'Cold outside?'

'Coldish.'

She took a sleek satiny jacket from the closet and sat down to brush her glossy hair.

'How much money have you got on you, Cliffy?'

I examined my wallet. 'About two hundred dollars.'

'How much can you draw from an ATM?'

'Fifteen hundred?'

'Got a cheque book on you?'

'Yes. Not much in the account.'

'A grand?'

I shrugged. 'I think so. Just.'

'Let's go. There's an ATM near the pub down the way and I'm due to meet someone there pretty soon. You give me two thousand seven hundred dollars and I'll answer your question. In fact, you're a life-saver. Give me fifty now.'

I gave her the note. She opened a drawer in the dressing table, took out a small pillbox and tapped out some white powder. She folded the note and pushed the powder around into two lines. Then she rolled the note tightly and used it to snort both lines. She sniffed, wet her finger to pick up the residue and licked the finger. She smiled at me and put the money in her pocket.

'Let's go.'

We left the house and walked down the street to where there was an ATM on one corner and a pub on the other. I drew out the money and we crossed and went into the pub. Kelly gave a thumbs-up to a man leaning on the bar, but took a seat in another part of the room.

'Get me a large vodka and tonic with a slice of lemon and we'll talk business.'

I went to the bar. The man she'd signalled to gave me a brief knowing look before returning his attention to the racing section in the newspaper spread out in front of him. His fingers were heavily nicotine-stained and his hand trembled as he turned the page. I got Kelly's vodka and a glass of white wine for myself.

'Your dealer?' I said as I put the glasses down.

'Got it in one. I was broke and was going to have to talk him into letting me have some on credit. Not now.'

'Not yet,' I said. I made a pile of the notes and put my cheque book on top of them. 'Who do I make the cheque out to?'

'Cash, of course. Hey, I've just realised. You're working. Who for?'

I shook my head.

'You're on expenses.'

'Forget it, Kel. This is it, there ain't no more, that fifty won't get you far. He might let you have some blow if you blow him.'

'How about if I blow you?'

'We've been through that.'

'Okay, write the cheque.'

I did and folded it and the cash together into a sizeable chunk. She eyed it hungrily.

'What did they talk about?'

Either she had built up a strong tolerance or the coke she'd taken was of low quality, because the high was leaving her minute by minute. She took a big slug of her drink, but it wasn't going to stop her coming down and she knew it.

'All right and fuck you. The prick said he was obeying orders.'

'Whose orders?'

'He didn't say. The cunt said that they should use me to find out the names of the politicians Rory had got to and what he had on them. He said no.'

'And he cut her throat for that?'

'No, there's more. You might get your kicks from this. He wanted us to get in a threesome. He wanted her to finger me while he fucked her, or the other way around. She wouldn't do it. She called him a pervert and he lost it and killed her.'

She finished her drink and reached for the money. Her hand stopped a bit short of it and she started to laugh, the most bitter laugh I could ever remember hearing.

'What?' I said.

'The funny thing is, I didn't know the names and I don't know about the dirt. She would've had to torture me and she'd have done it, the slant-eyed little cunt.'

'Who does know?'

'Who do you reckon? Rory and that treacherous blonde bitch.'

'Where are they?'

She snatched at the money. 'Fuck, you want everything, don't you?'

I pinned the money with my fist.

'Last I heard,' she said, 'they were in fucking Darwin.'

'Who told you that?'

'Glassop, that IT nerd. I met him at a sort of party in a wine bar. He was splashing money about and I helped to get him pissed and tapped him for a hundred bucks. He thought he might get into my pants. Some hope. He told me he helped them get tickets under false names.'

I let her grab the money. She shoved it in a pocket, got up and almost lost her balance in her high heels.

'You need help, Kelly,' I said.

'Fuck you. Like you care. I'm helping myself. Tell you one thing, arsehole. You're not the first to come looking.'

'Who else?'

'Work it out.'

She tottered to the bar to make her connection.

10

I went online to look for stories about O'Hara and Penelope
Milton-Smith. There had been a few, with photographs,
from around the time of the police investigation into Kelly
Scott's abduction and the death of Melanie Kim. Apart
from one picture of them onstage at Wollongong, they were
paparazzi shots with both subjects trying to avoid being
photographed. There was one photo of them together, both
dressed down and wearing shades, on a city street, but there'd
been nothing for nearly a month. I was wondering about
their relationship when Colin Williamson rang.

'I haven't got much,' he said.

'Every little helps.'

'I talked to a guy who was sitting in on one of the interviews
with O'Hara. He wasn't the main man, but heard quite a bit.
He said O'Hara was very nervous and very uncooperative.'

'You're not his favourite people.'

'Yeah, but on the basis of that they put a surveillance team on him and the girlfriend and this guy was part of that team. He says it was weird. They spotted the team and did everything to make it easy for them. Like they welcomed them.'

Welcomed the protection, I thought. 'That's interesting.'

'If you say so. But what's more interesting is that they eventually took advantage of being such easy targets and our guys getting slack and managed to dodge the team. Haven't been picked up since. They're in the wind.'

That needed some thought. Who were Rory and Pen in need of protection, and then in hiding, from? Presumably whoever Sean Bright had been working for, and who the hell was that? Harry Jacobs didn't seem a likely candidate. His object seemed to have been to stop the O'Hara tour and that had been achieved. I liked the idea of the catalyst being O'Hara's announcement of his political connections. That suggested one or more of the people he'd had undertakings from had had second thoughts. It all pointed to a need to get information from O'Hara and Pen. Melanie Kim's death was beginning to look like collateral damage.

I laid it out for Neville Kim in a Macquarie Street coffee shop, putting my theory about Melanie Kim's wish to exploit the situation as delicately as I could. He drank a long black while listening without interruption.

'Foolish, foolish girl,' he said when I'd finished. 'It fits though. She would have enjoyed being at the centre of a media and political storm. Despite all the sleaziness—no, partly because of it, she would have felt she had scored against the family. Who was it said that all families are unhappy?'

'I'm not sure,' I said. 'A Russian, I think. The thing is, Mr Kim, this is blowing up into something much bigger than it looked at first. I've already paid out quite a lot of money to—'

'Are you saying it's too big for you?'

'No.'

'I assure you it's not too big for me. Go to Darwin, go wherever you have to to find who killed my sister.'

'And what about whoever may have been behind it?'

He shrugged his well-tailored shoulders. 'My chief concern is the actual killer. If the net spreads further that will be interesting but probably no concern of mine and therefore no concern of yours unless you want it to be. I have confidence in you, Mr Hardy.'

'Thank you.'

'The funds are available. Use them.'

They were the best terms I'd ever had from a client on the basis of a preliminary report. O'Hara and Pen had gone just about as far away in Australia as you could go without needing a passport, but, luckily, I had a useful contact in the Top End.

A long-time friend, Harry Tickener, was the editor of the *Sentinel,* an online magazine dedicated to printing what the mainstream media shied away from. He had a stringer, Dave Burns, whom I'd met a few times.

Dave was a Tiwi Islander and the only indigenous person with a PIA licence, as far as I knew. For Harry, he kept a close watch on the asylum seekers held in detention in Darwin and the Indonesian fishermen held in gaol. He was something of a celebrity—related to a good many of the Tiwi Islanders who played Australian football locally, as he had himself, and in the big league. He was also a major figure in the organisation of the Arafura Games, a competition that attracted athletes from all over the world. Harry had told me Dave had been courted by political parties of all persuasions and had knocked them all back.

I got his number from Harry, rang him, got his answering machine, left a message and he rang back an hour later.

'Cliff Hardy,' he said. 'I heard you lost your licence?'

'I found it again. I'm looking for someone up your way, Dave. Think you could help? Have you got some time?'

'Is it urgent?'

I thought of Kelly's parting remark. 'It could be.'

'I've got the time if you've got the money.'

'It so happens I do.'

I booked the ticket, the hire car and the hotel online. Good time to go to the Territory—the Dry, with the temperature usually steady around thirty degrees. I packed a bag—light clothes, swimmers, a hat, camera and voice recorder, no gun, impossible on a domestic trip—and caught a morning flight.

Don't eat much, don't drink, and get up and walk to avoid DVT are the recommended rules. I obeyed two of them, slept a bit and read about opium and how the British had created millions of Chinese addicts in the interest of trade. There were case histories of people, some of whom did very well on the drug and others who went insane.

Darwin was warm and breezy under a clear sky. The flight had taken a little under four hours and there was only a half-hour difference between Sydney and Darwin so that it was just before midday when I arrived, collected my hired Pajero and drove to Palmerston, Darwin's satellite city, where Dave Burns had an office. I had the address and the GPS took me there. Dave's place turned out to be a demountable, one of a number perched on a dusty block in a light industrial area on the northern outskirts.

I parked just about at the demountable's door. The 4WD had squeaky brakes and the engine was running a bit roughly. Alerted by the noise, Dave opened the door and was standing at the top of the steps leading to it before I could get out of the car.

'Hi, Cliff,' he said. 'You need a mechanic not a private eye. That thing has problems.'

'Gidday, Dave. It'll do.'

I got out, carrying an A4 manila envelope. He came down the steps and we shook hands. Tall and rangy, Dave was in his early forties but looked as if he could still take a mark and kick a goal if required. We went into his office, which was hot with no air-conditioning, cramped and smelled of tobacco smoke. Dave wasn't a smoker but most of his indigenous clients were and in that climate, moist for a good part of the year, the smell soaked into paper and the furniture. Not that there was much of that—a desk, two filing cabinets, two chairs.

Dave was in shorts, sandals and an untucked polo shirt; I felt overdressed in drill trousers, shoes and a long-sleeved shirt.

'So what brings the big smoke to the Top End?'

'Looking for someone, Dave.'

I'd made copies of the best photos I could find of O'Hara and Penelope Milton-Smith, including the one onstage during the Wollongong appearance where they both had a kind of celebrity performance glow. I took the copies from the envelope and passed them to him.

He shuffled them. 'Rory O'Hara,' he said. 'Who's the woman?'

I told him.

'Should be easy to find, looking like that.'

'I doubt she is now. Probably more like in that one in the street,' I said. 'I think they're in hiding.'

'From?'

I shrugged. 'Hard to say, but at the moment, as far as I'm concerned, from me. Here's the background.'

I filled him in thoroughly on the case. He was one of those people who didn't fidget, didn't scratch himself; you knew you had his full attention.

'Where do people hide up here?' I asked.

'In the bush or on a boat. Are either of them boaties?'

'Not that I know of.'

'There's various places around, out of town but not too far out, available for short-term rent. Sort of package deal— house, car, pool, camping gear, dog, the works. Most of the booking's done online but the places advertise with pamphlets. I've got a contact at the tourist bureau who might be useful. The bureau sort of hosts some of the places' websites.'

'Would money help?'

'Always.'

'I'm on a good wicket there. Neville Kim wants it done and he'll pay what it takes. That covers you, too.'

There was a light breeze through a set of louvred windows but I wasn't acclimatised and was sweating. Dave looked as if he'd just had a shower. He'd sat virtually still behind his desk to this point; now he turned on his computer and touched some keys.

'Better make it official, Cliff. You're enlisting me as an associate for this case?'

'Right.'

He printed out a form. 'Just one thing. If we find the guy who killed the girl, what d'we do?'

'Why are you asking?'

'I know you, or I know about you. I know you've taken a couple of people out and you tried to shoot the bloke who killed your girlfriend a while back. Where did Mr Kim draw the line?'

I shook my head. 'Nothing like that, Dave. Those shootings were in self-defence and once in hot blood. This is just a job, pure and simple. Straight to the cops if we even get a sniff of Sean Bright.'

He passed the form across and I signed it with a damp hand.

'I'm booked in at the Capricornia in Darwin,' I said. 'I'll check in, have a swim and try to get used to being back in summer again. Give me your bank details.'

Dave rose smoothly to his feet. 'Let's see how it goes.'

'I'd rather—'

'You whitefellas don't always get what you'd rather. Tell you what, I'll make a start today and we could talk this evening. How'd you like to see some boxing? I know you were into it. He touched his eyebrows where he didn't have white scars from boxing cuts but I did.

'Sure.'

'There's a card tonight at the Kingfisher pub, eight-thirty. It's on the harbour. You'll find it.'

We shook hands again and I drove into Darwin where Santa hadn't made it in 1974.

* * *

The Capricornia was only a block away from the CBD and the harbour was across the street, fringed by a park. The designer of the hotel seemed to have been unable to make up his mind between a desert oasis and a tropical island, but it was comfortable enough with a good-sized room, air-conditioning, mini-bar and a fan-cooled balcony. The pool was only a few metres away and I was in it within minutes of arriving.

Refreshed and more comfortable in shorts, a T-shirt and sandals, I sat out with a beer and had some crisps and a couple of the complimentary pieces of fruit for a late lunch. I was uncomfortable with Dave Burns's perception of me as a killer. Anyway, it was certainly not on the agenda now. I had no gun and this was primarily an information-gathering exercise.

I took a long walk around the city and out past Parliament House and down to the harbourside precinct. I'd never been there before and had to admit to being a bit disappointed. The CBD, with its shops, pubs and restaurants, had a homogenised look, and the official buildings and sleek tourist-oriented developments reminded me of Canberra. The populace was not as multi-ethnic as I'd imagined: a great many pale skins and freckles.

The most impressive thing about the place was the harbour. It stretched away to the far distance, slowly heaving with the calmness of the day. I thought it'd be more fun to be looking for O'Hara and Pen out on the water, although I wasn't a boatie either.

* * *

I'd bought a map on my walk and plotted my route to the Kingfisher pub. I got there early to have a meal and a drink—steak sandwich and salad and a rough red. The pub was on the harbour to the east of the city with a huge beer garden that ended in a thick stand of mangroves.

The crowd was mixed, the way boxing crowds always are, with men in smart lightweight suits and women in party dresses mingling with the T-shirted, tracksuited types. The ring was set up under lights outside in the centre of the beer garden. Twenty dollars admission and a stamp on the hand for coming and going to the bar and the toilet.

Now I did see the ethnic mix I'd expected. At least a third of the patrons were indigenous and there was a strong Asian presence—Chinese, Indonesians, at a guess, and Indians. Rock music was blasting up into a starry sky and night birds swooped, scoring hits on the insects attracted to the lights.

I paid, got my stamp and hung around near the gate to the beer garden waiting for Dave. Soon after 8 pm he appeared, dressed much as he'd been before but in white jeans rather than baggy shorts, accompanied by a woman he introduced as Tania Hope. She was dark but several shades lighter than Dave. She wore a light sleeveless dress. Makeup, jewellery and trimmings she didn't need; she was stunning just as she was.

Dave had an ice bucket with a bottle in it in one hand and three glasses in the other. We went through the gate and he and Tania nodded to people they knew as we worked our way to a table two rows back from the ring.

'Tania worries about the blood,' Dave said. 'How d'you feel about that, Cliff?'

'I only worry when it's mine.' I smiled at Tania. 'Sorry, I can't resist when someone plays the straight man for me.'

'Blokes,' she said. 'Let's have a drink.'

Dave poured the chilled white wine and we chatted as the crowd built up quickly and the noise mounted. Smoking was permitted in the open and a blue haze was caught in the lights. Then the lights suddenly blacked out for about ten seconds and when they cane back on, the officials and the announcer were in the ring.

It was a six-fight card—four three-rounders, a six-round preliminary and a ten-round main event. Most of the fighters were black and they'd had extensive amateur careers so that they knew what they were doing in the ring. Two of the early fights ended in draws and two were stopped at the first sign of a man in trouble. The crowd grew a bit restless at what it saw as tame stuff but the two preliminary fighters, welterweight, one white one black, gave them all the action they could have asked for. The heavy-hitting white man wore his opponent down after four rounds of fierce fighting and the bout was stopped in the fifth after the black man had been downed twice.

The grog was flowing and I noticed a couple of very big men, bouncers, issuing warnings to some tables that threatened to reproduce the ring action out among the bottles and glasses.

'That job pays well,' Dave said, 'but there are certain requirements of height, weight and willing.'

We were pacing ourselves with the wine. I took a modest sip. 'Have you done it?'

'Once only.'

Two heavyweights in the main event, a tall light-skinned Aboriginal with tattoos that darkened his arms, and a stocky Torres Strait Islander. Both had their supporters and the noise level rose as they went to work. They felt each other out for the first few rounds, to the crowd's disapproval, and then fell into their natural fighting patterns—the taller man jabbing, retreating, the bulkier Islander bustling, trying to get in close. Not too much damage was done until the seventh round when the Aboriginal reeled away from a clinch with a cut above his eye streaming blood. The referee deemed it the result of a head clash and the bout was declared a draw. No one was happy in or out of the ring and the bouncers were busy breaking up altercations among the spectators.

We sat until the crowd began to thin and as I got up I looked across to where people were filing out through the gate. A man felt for something in the pocket of his light jacket. His face was caught in the light. He had a trimmed dark beard and his hair was thin in front. He blinked, shaded his eyes, then moved forward. He limped slightly and I recognised Rory O'Hara.

11

There was no chance of getting closer to O'Hara. He was through the gate before I could move and there were clutches of people in my way, including a bunch being calmed down by one of the bouncers. Dave noticed my reaction.

'What?' he said.

'I saw O'Hara.'

'Are you sure?'

I thought about it as we moved towards the gate. It was only a flash but I felt certain. I remembered how he'd arranged his hair to conceal the incipient widow's peak that was now evident. Same height, same build; the short beard didn't alter the cast of his features and the slight limp to adjust his balance was exactly the way O'Hara had moved when he was on the stage in Wollongong and had taken, dramatically, some steps without his stick.

'It was him.'

'Who was who?' Tania said.

We went through the gate and out to the car park. I invited them back to the Capricornia for a drink.

'You know I said I had a contact in the tourist office,' Dave said. 'This is it, or her, or she, or whatever.'

I said, 'Tania, I'm up here looking for someone.'

'Dave told me that much.'

'You might be able to help,' I said. 'Let's have a drink and talk about it.'

The car park at the Capricornia was almost full but Dave found a space for his Holden ute. We went to the bar; Dave and I opted for light beers, Tania had a bitter lemon.

'Designated driver,' she said.

'Are they tough on DUI up here?' I said.

They exchanged glances and laughed. 'They are for certain categories of person,' Tania said.

I gave Tania the essentials, stressing that I only wanted to talk to the people I was looking for and that there was nothing heavy involved.

Dave said, 'Did he see you?'

'No. He was caught in the light. I was well back, in the dark.'

'What if they don't want to talk to you?' Tania said.

'I can be persuasive.'

'I bet you can. Well, if it was the right guy you saw that helps a lot.'

'How's that?' I said.

Tania touched Dave's arm. 'How far would you travel to get to a fight night like that one?'

Dave shrugged. 'No top-liners, pretty ordinary stuff. Fifty klicks? Not much more.'

'There you are,' Tania said. She put one index finger on the table and drew a semicircle around it with the other. 'There's your target area. You say these people have money?'

'Yes,' I said.

'That narrows it. I can give you a list of the likely places within the zone.'

I looked at Dave. 'I should've gone straight to her,' I said.

Dave smiled. 'I facilitated.'

By noon the following day Tania had come good with a list of eight 'homestay' places within a hundred kilometres of the city that had been rented inside the past two months. The tourist office had been advised that the places had been taken off the market until further notice but had not been given any details about the bookings.

Dave and I took four each. The idea was that Dave would think up some excuse to call at the property, meet the lessees and report to me if he hit paydirt. If I found the right place, I'd let him know to stop looking and I'd talk to O'Hara and Penelope and try to find out what was going on, why they were hiding and what that implied about the killing of Melanie Kim.

Dave covered two places the first day with no hits. I only made it to one—a five-acre tract that had been part of a banana plantation—an hour's drive to the west on a hard surface and as much again on an unmade road. Nice house, up on stilts Queenslander-style, with a pool and a tennis court and all the privacy you could wish for. A lesbian couple were in residence; that is to say, they were in the pool and they didn't invite me to join them.

On my way to the next stop the Pajero broke down. I had a long, hot wait until the hire firm sent a tow truck with a mechanic who failed to solve the problem. I had a short-tempered, jolting ride back to the Darwin depot.

'Told you,' Dave said when I phoned him mid-afternoon to let him know what had happened.

'Yeah, well, they're giving me another one tomorrow. I'm too buggered to do any more today.'

'Getting old, Cliff.'

'But getting meaner, that's what gives me my edge. Talk to you tomorrow. How's Tania?'

'Eager for results.'

'Aren't we all?'

In the morning the car-hire firm told me they now wouldn't have a suitable vehicle for another day, so we decided to team up until then. Dave's ute was a 4WD and it handled the off-road well. We called in at two homestays without success—a grey-nomad foursome taking a break and a honeymoon couple who couldn't wait for us to leave.

A bit after 1 pm we pulled into a service station in a one-horse town right at the limit of our search area. There was a place to check nearby and another we could visit on the way back. I paid to fill the Holden's tank and for sandwiches and coffee. We sat at a table under a big tree, batting away flies.

Dave walked off into the scrub and came back with a handful of green berries. He demonstrated how to crush them and rub the juice over the face and arms. The flies stayed away.

'Natural Aerogard,' Dave said.

'You should patent it.'

'Thing is, it doesn't last long and people with sensitive skin break out in blisters.'

'Now you tell me.'

'You? Sensitive skin? Looked at yourself in the mirror lately?'

'I try not to.'

Dave studied the brochure for the next place on our list—Happy Springs. 'Says it's got a natural spring, rainforest in a sort of valley, wildlife. Sounds all right.'

I slapped at a fly. 'Buggers are back. How far is it?'

'Not far. Two ways to get there—scenic route through some sandhill country or direct.'

'I've seen sandhills, let's go direct.'

We tidied up and drove for ten minutes before leaving the tarmac and running along a graded dirt road with spinifex scrub on either side.

'This'd be a bog in the Wet,' Dave said. 'Cattle'd do all right here for a while.'

'What about camels?'

He laughed. 'They do all right anywhere.'

After twenty minutes or so we entered a bowl-shaped landscape that seemed to have trapped some of the moisture of the wet season. The scrub was greener and dotted with a few sizeable trees. We went over a long, gently sloping rise and down into a narrow valley with still taller trees. The mid-afternoon sun glanced off a set of iron roofs. Getting closer we could see several buildings and cleared areas with clusters of palm trees.

'Shangri-la,' I said. 'Shouldn't this all be Aboriginal land?'

'There's excised bits that don't get talked about much.'

We drove down a well-maintained gravel road to a gate standing open in a high cyclone fence that ran away in both directions into lush bush. Past the gate the gravel gave way to a cement drive that swept around a corner and led to two buildings connected by a covered breezeway. The blue shimmer of a swimming pool was visible away to the right. The buildings, fringed by palm trees, were long and low with wide verandas in front.

'My kind of place,' Dave said.

He ran the ute into a three-station carport where a near

new Nissan Patrol stood, or rather slumped. Its tyres had been slashed back and front.

'It's too quiet,' I said.

Dave turned the engine back on and blew the horn three times. There was no response apart from some birds taking off from the trees.

'What now?' Dave said.

'Proceed with caution.'

We approached the larger of the buildings, used the door knocker and heard the dead sound that comes from an empty house. I took off the cap I was wearing and used it to turn the door knob.

We went into a large open space, lit by wide windows and seeming to be a sitting room, kitchen, dining and games area all in one. There were modern conveniences in the kitchen, comfortable-looking cane chairs with cushions, a well-stocked bar and a darts board and pool table. CD set-up, wide-screen TV with a DVD player and a shelf packed with discs for both machines. A fan set to medium speed whirred softly overhead in the main room.

Three doors led off the room. I opened them the way I had the front door: bathroom and two bedrooms, not tidy, not untidy, just like the main room and just as empty.

We went out the way we'd come in and down some steps at the end of the veranda to the breezeway. Halfway along, Dave grabbed my arm and pointed towards the swimming pool.

'What?' I said.

'You blind bloody whitefellas.' He was off, running towards the pool fence, and I followed. The gate was open. When I got closer I could see Dave bending over a figure stretched out on a banana lounge.

'This is your guy,' Dave said as I joined him.

'Is he dead?'

Dave laughed. 'In a way. He's dead drunk.'

Rory O'Hara was naked, deeply tanned all over and snoring. An area around his left temple was bruised and an abrasion on his face had begun to scab over. A walking stick lay beside the banana lounge with a glass tumbler and an empty bottle of Jack Daniel's.

12

'Chuck him in the pool?' Dave said.

'Probably not cool enough to do any good.'

A towel lay under the lounge. I got it thoroughly wet in the pool and spread it over O'Hara's face and chest. After a few seconds he spluttered. Then he lapsed back into snoring. I lifted the towel, held it over his head and wrung it out so that the water fell on his face and open mouth. He spluttered again but this time his eyes opened and he spat, struggling to get rid of the taste of warm chlorinated water.

I draped the towel over him and ratcheted up the back of the lounge so that he was forced into a sitting position.

'Hello, Rory,' I said. 'Did you enjoy the fights?'

He groaned. 'Jesus, she was right.'

He clutched at the towel and reached for the bottle.

'Empty, mate,' Dave said.

'Who the fuck are you?' O'Hara snarled.

'He's with me,' I said, 'and we've got some questions for you and Penelope.'

O'Hara's chapped lips formed a kind of smile. He plucked self-consciously at his retreating hairline. 'Good luck with half of that,' he said.

We hauled him to his feet and walked him around the pool for a few minutes. Then he slid in at the shallow end and splashed about, spluttering and coughing. He got out, wrapped the towel around himself and looked at me.

'Questions, you said.'

'That's right.'

'Better come inside. I need coffee.'

'Got a beer?' Dave said.

'I've got everything, Mr . . .?'

'Burns, Dave Burns.'

'I've got everything, Mr Burns . . . and nothing.'

O'Hara showered and dressed in stylish cargo shorts and a T-shirt while Dave and I drank Crown lager. O'Hara brewed up a pot of coffee, poured himself a full mug and didn't offer us any. He was rapidly recovering some of his silver spoon superiority, but only some.

'What are you doing here, Hardy?'

Fair question. I told him. He sipped his coffee and gave what I'd said some thought. He'd slicked his hair back and looked older and more vulnerable with the widow's peak revealed. There were jowls developing and the beginnings of slack skin under his eyes.

'Who'd have thought it?' he said. 'The poor little nursie had clout. I guess that could've been their first mistake.'

'You're going to have to explain that, Rory.'

'They weren't to know that killing her would put a blood-hound on their trail. So you're going after them?'

'Not them, just Bright.'

'It's bigger than him but you're a bit late. He was here.'

'When was this? How long was he here and how did he find you?'

'How did you?'

'I spotted you at the boxing.'

'So did he and he followed me back. He was only here about, oh, the rest of that night and most of yesterday. It was enough.'

'Where's Pen?'

'He took her.'

His attitude angered me. He seemed passive, resigned, and his eyes kept straying to the bar. Was this the same man as the one who'd blown the whistle on a multi-million dollar scam and captivated a big audience in Wollongong? I shot him a barrage of questions.

'Have another beer,' he said. 'Have a few, it's going to take a while to make you understand what's been going on.'

O'Hara said that one member of the Greens, two ALP members and three in the Coalition had given him assurances of support if he formed a political party.

'What's important is the people behind them. Two of the conservatives and one of the ALP men are completely beholden to certain business interests. They are their creatures, as they'd have been called in the old days.'

'I'm guessing mining companies,' Dave said.

'That's right, you're guessing.'

What I most wanted to hear about was what had happened to Pen but it was important to keep him talking. I judged that he didn't care about her, probably didn't care much about anything. Pen had asked me if I thought he was a cipher: he was now. 'What about the Green and the other ALP guy— or is it a woman?'

O'Hara smiled. 'Good try. Idealists, genuine idealists.'

'So Bright was acting for one of these interests,' I said. 'Protecting their investment. Keeping an eye out and grabbing Kelly to get some leverage when you went public?'

'That's right.'

O'Hara suddenly looked even more diminished, maybe close to contrite.

'Hold on,' I said. 'How would the people pulling the politicians' strings know they'd been privately in discussion with you?'

O'Hara sighed. 'That's where I played the wrong card. I ... contacted certain people and asked them for money. I was a bit desperate but I didn't let it show. I pulled out all the stops, gave them my A game. This was before Jack came up with the idea of the tour and the film and everything. I mentioned certain names.'

Dave shook his head and O'Hara made a move as if to hit him but quickly thought better of it.

'Okay, I was stupid then and stupid again. I jumped the gun. Stupid. I thought I needed to do something to attract attention to the tour. I needed the publicity and the money. Pen advised me against it, just like she . . .'

'What?' I said.

'Told me not to go to the boxing. We had a row. I was getting cabin fever.'

'Nice cabin,' Dave said.

O'Hara sneered. 'I've had nicer.'

'Go on,' I said.

O'Hara drew in a deep breath and drained his coffee mug. He glanced around and I knew what he was looking for.

'No more grog, Rory,' I said. 'Not just now. Let's hear the rest.'

'I'm only guessing, but I reckon Bright recruited the Korean girl to play the nurse, and they had a falling out when they'd got Kelly away.'

'I think that's right,' I said. 'As you say it's guesswork, but the signs are that Melanie Kim wanted to pressure Kelly for the names, go public and be a media sensation.'

O'Hara nodded. 'That sounds right. Wouldn't have fitted Bright's brief at all and, anyway, Kelly didn't know the names.'

'Who does, apart from you?'

'The point is, who's got the evidence—the dates, the places, the times, the voice messages, the emails . . .?'

'The people you had undertakings from can't be that dumb,' Dave said.

'They didn't know that I was documenting everything. And they were desperate. Politicians are always manoeuvring and they know when their days are numbered. The right move by those three could save their careers.'

'Not now,' I said.

'No, I'm on the nose now, but they'll be shitting themselves and so will their ... sponsors. If those politicians go down they'll want to take people with them.'

Dave was sceptical. 'What can they do?'

'You don't understand politicians. They're snakes, treacherous bastards, that's how they get where they are. They know people have the dirt on them and they fucking get as much dirt as they can back. They boast about it; they give you hints.'

'And you were ready to deal with them. What happened to the tribune of the people?'

O'Hara refilled his mug. He drank some coffee that must have been lukewarm but he didn't seem to care. He shook his head as if he were dismissing his whole activist reputation and career. 'The tribune had a lot of money, then he didn't. That made the difference.'

Dave waved his hand at the room. 'This costs a bit.'

'It's all on Penelope's dime,' O'Hara said. 'She had some cash hoarded. Don't ask me why. Anyway, she's got all that compromising stuff stashed somewhere in Sydney. We knew the people behind Bright would come looking for us so we did the flit to here to lie low, let things cool down and think what to do next. Pen persuaded Gordon Glassop to get us false IDs. He didn't take much persuading. He asked for some money, not a lot.'

I nodded. 'Not a bad plan, but you left too much of a trail.'

'Yeah. Bright must have known that I liked boxing and looked for me there. Shit, he was intimidating. All he wanted to know about was the evidence. He had a gun and a nasty-looking knife. He scared the shit out of me and he . . .'

'What?'

'He came on to Penelope, I remember that.'

'What d'you mean, you remember?'

O'Hara dropped his head, stared into his empty mug. 'I've been drinking a lot. I was in AA for a while and got it under control but all this freaked me. I was more or less drunk when I went to the boxing. When I got back and he turned up I was pretty useless. I don't know what he did to Pen but she told him she had the evidence stashed. Bright bashed me and when I woke up they were gone.'

'So you took off your clothes and got really drunk?'

'I told you I freaked. What else was there to do?'

'Are you saying she went willingly?'

He shrugged and the action hurt him and resparked the anger in me. He touched the side of his head and closed his eyes briefly. 'Women,' he said. 'How can you tell?'

'Stashed the evidence where?' I said.

'No idea. She's a complete mystery to me.'

'What do you mean by that?'

'She just sort of arrived when I was starting on this new track. Just making noises. She sort of took over things, you know? The way women can. She really pushed things along, set up meetings, kept minutes, handled the tax side. I tried to screw her, of course, but no dice. Then Kelly happened along and I sort of enjoyed playing them off against each other.'

Dave gave a snort of disgust and got up to look out the window as some clouds came across and the light dimmed.

'In Wollongong she told me she was in love with you,' I said.

'Is that right? Clive told me she was giving Bright the eye back then. It looked to me as if she was interested in you.'

'You're painting her as a conspirator from the start.'

'I just don't know. Maybe.'

We sat in silence for a while with O'Hara sipping cold coffee, Dave tracing pictures with his finger in the dust on the window and me thinking hard.

'Okay, Rory. Who're the politicians and who're the sponsors?'

'Fuck you. I'm not going to tell you and I'm going to have a drink.'

I nodded. What did I care? I was focused now on Bright and Pen, nothing else. 'Before you do, who recommended Penelope to you?'

O'Hara limped to the bar. He'd recovered his stick and it tapped the floor. He slopped a big measure of Johnnie Walker Black Label into his coffee mug, took a long pull and raised the mug in a kind of salute.

'Jack Buchanan,' he said. 'Or Harry Jacobs, or both. I honestly forget. Won't do you any good though—Jack's a financial train wreck since he lost out big time in an arbitration and Jacobs took off for Israel the minute he came out on top. Presumably to thank Jehovah at the Wailing Wall.'

13

O'Hara had nothing more to add. I asked him what he was going to do next.

'What do you suggest?'

I couldn't think of anything to say and shrugged.

'Exactly,' he said, and added more scotch to his mug.

'He's a miserable piece of work,' Dave said as we drove away.

'Different man from the one I met at the beginning of this. He was brim-full of confidence, hot to trot.'

'Hard to believe. I'll ask you what you asked him—what're you gonna do?'

'Find Bright and the woman.'

Dave muttered something in his own language and I asked him what it meant.

'Big country,' he said.

* * *

I paid Dave his standard time rate and for his expenses—
use of his vehicle and advice. He told me he and Tania were
getting married at the end of the year and that I'd be invited.
'Where will you go for your honeymoon?' I asked.

'Bali, where else?'

I checked out of the Capricornia in the morning and
caught a noon flight back to Sydney. On the way I went over
everything I could remember of my contact with Penelope
Milton-Smith, which didn't amount to more than a few
hours in all. She'd said she would put Jack Buchanan at
the top of the list of people who might have had it in for
O'Hara because he had marketing rights on him and, like
Elvis and John Lennon, he'd be worth more dead than alive.
But that could've been disinformation.

She'd clearly known what O'Hara was going to say about
his political ambitions, but hadn't even given me a hint. I'd
thought she was sincere when she told me she was in love
with O'Hara but, as someone said—was it Richard Nixon?—
if you can fake sincerity you've got it made.

Pen's distress when Kelly was abducted seemed genuine
too, but that could have been faked as well, or a surprise
because it was an interruption to an earlier plan. She hadn't
come on to me in the slightest way, but she hadn't needed to.
I'd been attracted to her and when that happens the antennae
go down and you see and hear what you want to see and hear.

That led me to thinking about Bright, with whom I'd
scarcely had any contact at all. He'd pulled the wool over a

few people's eyes and shown himself to be resourceful and ruthless. But he'd also shown patience and restraint with O'Hara and it was uncertain quite how he'd handled Penelope. Ruthlessness and restraint were dangerous attributes in the one package. Combine that with the support of powerful business interests and it added up to a formidable opponent.

Back in Sydney, I had the uncomfortable task of reporting to Neville Kim. I didn't have much to show for his considerable outlay of funds except confirmation that politics and money lay behind the killing of his sister.

As before, we met over coffee in the city. He didn't seem overly disappointed.

'It would help to know the names of the politicians,' he said. 'Their connections could be traced.'

'Too hard the other way around.'

He smiled. 'True. We businessmen have to keep many channels open, and many tributaries to those channels. How do you propose to proceed?'

'You want me to go on, to look for a resourceful and well-financed man and a woman whose actions and motivations are a mystery?'

'Of course. Isn't that what you do?'

I said it was; what I didn't say was that it was about as big a challenge as I could remember facing.

Jack Buchanan. Things seemed to keep circling back to him and one thing was for sure—he hadn't been straight with me from the beginning. It was time to sort him out. His office was in Randwick; I knew he lived in one of the beachside suburbs but I didn't know which. I felt pretty sure that, after our last conversation, he wouldn't want to see me. But how strongly would he feel about that? I parked across from the exit to the car park under his office block and rang on my mobile.

'Mr Buchanan's office.'

'This is Cliff Hardy. I'd like to talk to Jack.'

'I'm sorry, Mr . . . Hardy, Mr Buchanan's not in the office today. Can I take a message?'

Her voice had the unmistakable tone of someone telling a pre-programmed lie.

'I'm sorry,' I said. 'I don't believe you. Tell him I'm in my office and he can call me there. If he doesn't, I'm coming to Randwick and I'm not in a good mood.'

She didn't respond and I hung up.

Ten minutes later Jack's silver Alfa emerged from the car park and headed east. Late afternoon traffic in the eastern suburbs is as heavy as anywhere else in Sydney, but it tends to be more polite—more women driving, and more people driving expensive cars they don't want to damage. Jack was an exception; he drove in an ill-tempered, stop-start fashion, bullying the women in the SUVs and competing with the men in the other up-market imports. The style really gains you no advantage; you tend to end up with your competitors at the same sets of light. But it made him easy to follow from back in the body of the traffic.

We were heading towards Bronte when my mobile rang. I had it slotted into the hands-free set-up and I answered.

'Mr Hardy, this is Kathy Mason, Mr Buchanan's secretary. I thought I should warn you. Mr Buchanan has been acting very strangely in the last few days and he bolted from the office after you rang and took a gun with him. I saw it.'

'Yes.'

'I don't know what to do.'

Somehow I forced a laugh. 'Jack was a stuntman, as you probably know. It won't be a real gun. I wouldn't worry. I'll call his mobile and I'll see him at home. We'll sort it out. I'll let you know what happens.'

'If you're sure . . .'

'I am.'

'He thinks a lot of you, Mr Hardy. He has a photo of the two of you on his wall.'

'Does he? Well, there you are. It'll be all right. Thank you, Kathy.'

The water came into view, sparkling under a blue-sky break in what had been an overcast day. The Alfa made a turn ahead of me and I was blocked off by a council truck backing slowly out of a lane. I fretted while the reversing signal bleeped at me. If there was anyone who knew his way with guns it was Jack. His gun would be the real thing, but why?

The Alfa pulled up in front of a semi-detached house in a quiet street a block back from the water. Jack got out of the car to unlock the gate so he could park in a paved area in front of the house. I pulled up behind him.

'Jack!'

He whirled around, his old instincts not forgotten, and whipped out a pistol.

'Don't move, Cliff. I swear I'll shoot you. They got to you, didn't they?'

'Who got to me? I don't know what you're talking about. I want to ask you stuff about O'Hara.'

'Have you got a gun?'

'No.'

'Show me.'

I turned out the linings of the pockets in my jacket and opened it to show him I had no shoulder holster. I turned around slowly so he could see I didn't have a gun in my belt at the back. If he was worried about an ankle gun he was even crazier than he seemed.

'Better put the piece away, Jack. Neighbours could be watching. You know how things are these days. They'd be on to the terrorist hotline in a flash.'

His pistol disappeared and he was the business-suited executive again, opening his gate.

'You came close then, Hardy,' he said. 'I've been under a lot of pressure. Anyway, I don't want to talk to you. Piss off.'

'You know me, Jack. I won't give you a minute's peace.'

'More gossip, is that what you want? I suppose you saw Kelly?'

'She was very helpful.'

'Fuck you. We'd better bloody get it over with.'

He drove in; I backed away and parked in the street. I followed him up a bricked path to the front of the house, staying a judicious distance away in case he tried one of his commando tricks. His shoulders were slumped as he fumbled with the door key. Not the Jack of old. The house had the cold, echoing feel of emptiness.

'Wife left when the judgment went against me, the bitch.'

His third or fourth wife. Nothing to say to that. We went down the passage, passing three doors, to a kitchen at the back of the house. There was a glassed-in sun porch beyond that and then a smallish paved courtyard.

'Say nice place and I'll pull out the gun and shoot you.'

'Take it easy, Jack,' I said. 'What made you think I'd been got at by someone? Who?'

He explained that he'd borrowed money to finance his legal battle with Harry Jacobs on the expectation that he'd win. He lost, and applied for more money to launch an appeal. That was refused and the original loan was being called in.

'Who by?' I said.

By this time we were sitting around a pine table in the kitchen drinking wine. Jack put his Glock on the table next to his glass.

'Some Lebs,' he said. 'You had dealings with them a few years ago, I heard.'

He was right. It was a tricky case involving a rogue cop, but it had left me at serious odds with a criminal Lebanese family, rather than allied with them, and I told Jack so.

He shrugged. 'You're for hire. I couldn't be sure. They're after me for the money, one way or another.'

I knew what he meant. There's all sorts of ways to threaten, coerce and use people. Suddenly Jack sat bolt upright in his chair.

'Where's Roxy?'

'Who?'

'My dog, she should . . .' He sprang up and bolted out through the sun porch door to the courtyard. I heard a low, agonised groan and when I got outside I found Jack sitting on the ground with a dog in his lap. It was a big dog, a German shepherd, light brown and black. A large pool of blood had spread over the crazy paving.

Jack rocked backward and forward.

'Those murdering wog bastards,' he moaned.

14

I'd owned three dogs in my young life and I remembered the pain of losing them. One, a terrific border collie-kelpie cross named Jem after Jem Ward, a gypsy bare-knuckle prize-fighter I'd read about, had been killed by a bull terrier and I'd had to be restrained by my father from taking a baseball bat to the culprit and its owner. Jack's dog had obviously been shot; two dark holes were visible in its light pelt, precisely placed to hit the heart. I glanced up and around. There were tall blocks of flats in three directions with clear views down into the courtyard.

I persuaded Jack to come back into the house. Got him some brandy and calmed him down. He was limp. Defeated.

'What am I going to do?'

'How much do you owe them?'

'A million plus.'

'What's this place worth?'

'A million five, around that. There's water views from two rooms built into the roof.'

'Do you own it outright?'

He nodded. 'From my big earning days.'

'What about the wife?'

He laughed. He'd drunk the first slug of Hennessy and was working on a second. 'We had a pre-nup. She's got more than me.'

'My advice would be to sell it, pay them, and start again.'

He glared at me, his eyes beginning to take on a malevolent glow. 'Is that what you did?'

'Not quite. Something like it.'

'You smug cocksucker. Sorry, didn't mean that. Probably good advice. I'm tired, Cliff. What was it you wanted from me?'

I asked him how Penelope Milton-Smith had got the job with O'Hara.

'I put her up for it,' he said. 'She was on my books as a motivational speaker. She was bloody good, too.'

'I imagine so. Did she ask for it?'

'Yeah, I think she did. Why?'

'Never mind. I have to find her. Can you think of anything she told you, or anything in her background that might help me?'

'You'd be wasting your time.'

'How's that?'

'She was bloody good-looking. Well, you know that.

I tried to make her but I got nowhere. I think she might be a dyke.'

'I want to find her, not fuck her.'

'Did you fuck Kelly?'

'No. Get your mind off sex. This is business.'

'You're a cold bastard when you want to be. All right, let me think. I remember a talk she gave to some corporate types about multiculturism. She said her parents had arrived from Greece without a word of English. They'd worked at all sorts of jobs, got some money together and opened a restaurant in . . . shit, where was it? Brighton-le-Sands, that's it.'

'So?'

'She said she grew up there, in a little flat above the restaurant that never made any money. Her father died, she said, and her mother kept the place going and still does. She said she sees her mother every week, or talks to her, without fail.'

'Was that true?'

'She's a great actress if it wasn't. She had them practically weeping.'

'Name of the restaurant?'

'Same as her maiden name, Marino . . . Marinos. That's it. Marinos.'

'Anything else?'

He shook his head and sucked down more brandy. 'Go away.'

* * *

It wasn't much but it was something. It was easy enough to locate the address of the restaurant on the Esplanade at Brighton-le-Sands. It had got dark while I was with Jack. I'm fond of Greek food; time to combine business with pleasure. I drove to the suburb, put the car in a massive parking station, bought a bottle of cleanskin white wine at Coles Liquorland and walked a block to the restaurant.

Marinos was small, wedged between a Lebanese take-out and a posh Chinese restaurant. It was half full and already noisy, the way Greek places often are where the cheerful atmosphere and good food tend to promote hilarity. The one waitress was busy and she waved me to a table for two, had a water bottle, tumbler and wine glass in front of me within a second or two and then vanished into the kitchen. She came out almost immediately, served a table of four, took an order at another table and vanished again. Megan, who'd done a fair bit of it, had told me that waiting was the wrong name for the job.

'It should be called foot-fucking,' she'd said and I could see what she meant.

When the waitress got to me I ordered grilled calamari for an entrée and sautéed liver for a main. The little place filled up. I paced myself with the wine and enjoyed the food. My target was obvious—a woman seated behind the cash register, handling the money and credit-card payments with grace and style. She was no black-clad widow; she wore an olive green silk blouse, muted but effective makeup, silver hoop earrings and her ash blonde hair was expensively cut and styled. She exuded warmth and I'd have bet more than a few of the restaurant's patrons were there just to have dealings with her.

I ordered coffee and wrote on the back of my business card that I was a friend of Penelope's and wanted to see her. I handed the card to the woman as I passed her desk on the way to the toilet. She nodded to me when I came back. The bill was on the table and I took it and my credit card to the desk.

'You say you are a friend,' she said as she processed the payment. Her English was very correct; her accent was heavy.

'That was an exaggeration, I admit. We ... worked together briefly before problems arose. Those problems still exist and I hope she can help me.'

She returned my card. 'My daughter badly needs a friend and she needs help herself.'

It was the first indication I'd had that Penelope wasn't on top of things all the time.

'I don't mean her any harm,' I said.

I stepped aside while she dealt with another customer.

'I watched you eat and drink,' she said. 'I watch everybody.'

'I'm sorry, I . . .'

'You can tell a lot from the way people eat and drink. I would say you were efficient.'

'Thank you. How about trustworthy?'

She smiled. 'That is harder to judge, but I think yes. Go back and take the stairs on the right. Be gentle with her.'

Her fingers flicked over the buttons on her mobile as she texted. I went up the stairs and found myself in a sitting room. A door to a kitchen was open; two other doors were closed.

'Pen?'

'In here.'

The voice, reedy, thin and muffled, came from behind one of the doors. I opened it and stepped inside the small bedroom. Penelope Milton-Smith was sitting in a chair by the single bed. The room was lit only by a low-voltage lamp and she was partly in shadow. She was wearing a faded dressing gown and even in the gloom I could see that her face was bruised and misshapen. There was a bandage around her neck and she held her left arm, with a cast on the wrist, awkwardly on a cushion. With her right hand she tossed a mobile phone onto the bed.

'Hello, Cliff.'

The voice was like a parody of her former confident modulated delivery.

'Jesus, Pen, what's happened?'

'He raped me,' she said. 'He bashed me and he raped me.'

15

Penelope broke down and cried. I put my arm around her and she pressed her face against me so I could feel her tears wetting my shirt. After a while she pulled a tissue from her dressing-gown pocket and wiped her eyes. Then she reached down to the floor and brought up first a bottle of vodka and then a glass. She poured a solid measure, the bottle tapping against the rim of the glass. She took a big swig and looked at me.

'I'm a mess,' she said.

'Not permanently,' I said.

She forced a smile. 'That's the only nice thing I've heard since . . .'

I sat on the bed. 'I went to Darwin. I saw Rory and he told me you'd left with Bright. Do you feel up to telling me what happened then?'

'Why?'

I explained that I was working for Melanie Kim's brother. Suddenly she seemed less interested in the vodka.

'You're going after him?'

'That's right.'

'What will you do if you catch him?'

'That'll depend on what he does. But I'll need help, Pen. I need to know everything about the material you have on the politicians and the people behind them.'

'Had,' she said. 'I kept thinking I could play him along and get away from him somehow but I couldn't. He threatened to scar me unless I gave him the files. He had this knife . . .'

Her hand shook and she spilled some of the vodka. I took the glass from her.

'Easy,' I said. 'He didn't scar you. You'll be beautiful again.'

Her eyes opened wide. 'I'm not beautiful.'

'If you ain't, you'll do till beautiful gets here.'

'That's from *No Country for Old Men*.'

'Right.'

She laughed and winced as the movement hurt her battered face.

'See?' I said. 'You're on the way back.'

'Christ, I think you're right. I've got to pull myself together. Help you? I'll do anything to get even with that bastard.'

She downed her drink, tossed the bottle onto the bed where it clicked against the mobile and stood up. She swayed but regained her balance and gave a triumphant grunt. Mrs Marinos came into the room.

'Darling, you're on your feet. That's much better.'

'Thank him, he's a good man.'

'It's about time you found one.'

'Don't start, Mama.'

They had a rapid-fire conversation in Greek.

'I've told her you're going to protect me. Are you?'

'Yes,' I said.

Pen went to the bathroom and tidied herself. She came back and I studied the books on the shelf while she got dressed. Moving slowly and carefully, it took time for her to work her way into a shirt, loose pants and a jacket. I helped her pull on a pair of dusty ankle boots.

'Haven't worn this gear in years,' she said. 'The stuff I arrived here in I never want to see again. He only let me bring my shoulder bag. Anyway, there were no other clothes to bring.'

'What happened to them? There was nothing left in Darwin, O'Hara said. Just some shoes.'

She put the dressing gown on a hook on the back of the door and leaned against the door for support. 'He ... cut it all up with his knife to show me how sharp it was. Specially the bras. He was a gentleman, though; he used a condom for the real fun.'

'Don't think about it.'

'I have to think about it. It keeps me angry.'

'Where do you want to go? Have you got a flat or something?'

'Sublet it when Rory and I took off.'

'Better come to my place.'

'No wife?'

'Right.'

'No partner?'

'Currently in LA and likely to stay there.'

'Let's go then.'

'How will your mother feel about that?'

'I'm thirty-six years old.'

'What did you tell her about your injuries?'

'What I told them at Casualty—that I fell down some stairs.'

'Did she believe you?'

'She pretended to. It's a relationship based on pretence. She lives in the old world.'

'She seems to be doing pretty well in the new one.'

'Men and money are her gods. She wanted a son.'

I helped her down the stairs. She spoke briefly to her mother in Greek. They kissed and we left the restaurant.

Responding to her questions, I initially did most of the talking on the drive to Glebe. I explained how seeing Kelly had led me to Darwin and how, under pressure, Jack Buchanan had helped me to find her. She wanted to know how O'Hara had been and I told her he was unsure whether she'd been involved in some sort of conspiracy from the start.

'Were you unsure?' she said.

'I had an open mind.'

'Poor Rory. He was all at sea and Bright terrified him. He tried to drink it all away. I can't talk, I wasn't much better. We made a great pair and Bright treated us like shit, which we deserved.'

'No you didn't.'

'We did. Rory lost his grip a while ago and I played along with him. He'd hooked those politicians and he planned to use them any way he could, but he was out of his league. I told him not to go public but all he had to work with was his charm and style by that stage. No money. He was scared.'

'Did you know he approached the people behind the politicians and tried to get money from them?'

'The stupid bugger. I told him not to do that. I didn't think he would. Shit, that could have set this whole thing off. Did he give you the names?'

'No. Did Bright ask for them?'

'No, he didn't seem interested. Maybe he knew already. All he wanted was the files, the evidence. He told us nothing.'

'Do you know who ran Rory down?'

She looked out the window and didn't answer. 'Where are we headed, Cliff?'

'Glebe.'

'Good, I like Glebe. Bright told us he did it to scare Rory off. At the time Rory thought it was an accident but he made a big thing of it as a warning to Buchanan and for publicity and all. That's where you came in.'

I turned into Glebe Point Road. 'There's an all-night chemist along here. D'you need anything?'

She patted the pockets of her jacket and yawned. 'I've got everything I need. A bath'd be good. Have you got a bath?'

'Yeah, and towels and a spare bed.'

'Heaven. Tomorrow I'll tell you everything I can.'

part two

16

I was in the kitchen making coffee when Pen came down the stairs. She was wearing a sweater Marisha had left behind with a few other things that I'd stowed away in the spare room.

'Nice sweater,' she said, 'and some other good stuff. Are you sure she isn't coming back for it any day now?'

'She was planning to outfit herself on Rodeo Drive. Coffee?'

'Please, and I'm starved.'

'I can do toast and poached eggs.'

She nodded and looked around the room. 'Not much of a woman's touch.'

I got the bread and eggs from the fridge. The bread was old but would be okay toasted. 'We were live-apart,' I said. 'Mostly.'

'Good idea.'

'How's the wrist?'

'Throbbing, but I've taken a couple of bombs. Who're the woman and the kid in the photo in the living room?'

'My daughter and grandson.'

'Lucky you.'

After we ate we took second mugs of coffee out into the bricked courtyard. There was a decent patch of winter sunlight that would last for a while. The garden furniture had seen better days but was still holding together.

Pen said that O'Hara, after resisting shakily for a short time, finally told Bright that she had what he wanted and that he didn't know where she'd hidden it. Under the threat of the knife, Pen told Bright where it was—in her car, which was in a lock-up garage in Bondi.

'He injected me with something that made me woozy but still able to function. He drove us back to Darwin and we got a flight to Sydney. I had my return ticket and he had one under another name.'

I said. 'What name?'

'I was doped. I'd have to think. We drove to Bondi. He had that bloody knife. My flat's in Bondi and I rent the garage a block away. I opened it and got the memory stick and a disk; the voice messages are on the disk and the emails and texts and all that are on the memory stick. They're encrypted but I had a laptop in the car and he made me give him the passwords so he could read the data.'

She was staring at the weeds forcing themselves through the brickwork. She'd finished her coffee and her hands, holding the still-warm mug, were shaking. She was living it again.

'He started to hit me and . . . handle me. He asked me if I had copies of the stuff. I said I didn't but he kept hitting me anyway. Then he opened the back door and held me down and almost suffocated me. Then he raped me . . . both ways. And he put the condom . . . in my mouth.'

I thought she was going to break down again and leaned towards her but she held me back and got control.

'He just left. Along the way he'd broken my wrist but I couldn't have driven anyway. I managed to get a cab to Casualty at the Prince of Wales. Then I went to Mama's.'

She put her mug down and plucked up a weed from between the bricks.

'Now you want to know about the people Rory dealt with.'

'When you're ready.'

'I'm ready.'

'First off, who did all the digital work?'

'I did. Most of it. Glassop revised it and helped me with tricky bits. Back then I'd have done pretty much anything Rory asked me to do. It was playing dirty but I thought it was justified then.'

The sun had gone behind the flats next door. The shade is welcome in summer but not in winter. The temperature dropped suddenly and we went inside. Pen asked for paper and she made a list of the politicians O'Hara had some kind of undertakings with. She confirmed O'Hara's statement that one National, one Liberal and one ALP member were in the pay of powerful business interests and handed me the list:

Barry Cartwright—ALP
Simon Featherstone—National
Timothy Polkinghorn—Liberal

'Alphabetical,' I said. 'I was hoping you would list them in the order of most likely.'

She shrugged. 'I simply don't know. One thing I do know is that they dislike each other pretty intensely and none of them knows about the other. Rory was very amused by that.'

'How about the business interests?'

She took the paper back and added to it. Cartwright represented an inner-city electorate in Melbourne and had ties to developers; Featherstone's rural electorate was in northern New South Wales and he was hand-in-glove with coal-seam gas companies; Polkinghorn had close ties with an internationally based merchant bank.

'Is this stuff well known?' I asked after I'd read the notes.

'God, no. Rory paid a hell of a lot of money to find it out. That was one of the big drains on his resources.'

'I can't see what they'd have to gain by throwing in with O'Hara.'

'Their seats are vulnerable, apparently. Rory was promising massive publicity for them as members of his party and he claimed to be able to use social media the way Barack Obama did and change the political landscape. If it worked they'd have got in to the new order of things on the bottom floor. You have to understand how persuasive he could be before he lost his mojo.'

I'd seen that at work but I still wasn't convinced. 'Do you think he blackmailed them once he had the dirt on them?'

'I don't think so, but that's not to say he wouldn't have. There'd be no point now. There's not a shred of proof now and all the background research into the connections Rory paid for has gone, too. The providers wouldn't do it again.'

The exercise had exhausted her and she went upstairs for a rest. I sat with the notes in front of me. Simple problem: find which of the business interests would be most worried about O'Hara's intentions. Worried enough to hire someone like Bright to take drastic action. Problem simple, solution difficult.

I left Pen a note and a key. I went to the gym for an overdue workout and felt the pain that comes from trying to do the exercises you used to do after a period of neglect. Wes Scott, the owner and trainer, watched me and shook his head.

'I know,' I said. 'I've been busy.'

'Like I said once before, man, Rookwood's full of busy guys not busy now.'

I stopped on the way home for food and wine. When I got in I could hear computer keys being tapped in the spare room. I put the supplies away, thought about going up to see what she was doing but decided to leave her to it.

I rang Neville Kim, told him I'd located Pen and was working towards finding a target.

'A target would be a good thing,' he said. 'When you have one, let me know. I might be able to help.'

Dave Burns rang to tell me that O'Hara had left Darwin. The owners of Happy Springs had complained that the lessee, Mr Marinos, had left the house and pool in a disgraceful state. The tourist office took note. Dave had a contact at the airport, who told him Roger Marinos had flown to Sydney the previous day. I thanked him and asked if he'd decided on the wedding date.

'Working on it. How's the investigation going?'

'Trying to fix on a target.'

'A target, I like it.'

Everybody liked it; the job was to find it.

I heard the printer clicking and after a while Pen came down with a sheaf of papers in her hand.

'This is all I can remember of the background stuff. The three pollies and their corporate mates and their connections. I can't remember the texts and emails exactly but this is the gist of it. I'm sure there are gaps. It's been a while since I dealt with it all and . . . a lot's happened.'

'That'll be a big help. How're you feeling?'

'A bit better and I'd like a drink. I drink too much as you've probably noticed.'

'Who doesn't? I've bought some wine and there's some scotch. Nothing much else.'

'Wine,' she said. 'Plenty of wine and you can go through this stuff with your experienced and analytical mind and prioritise the investigation.'

'Are you taking the piss?'

She shook her head. 'Just feeling sorry for myself when I should've been feeling sorry for that poor girl. I've had a bad time but she . . . and I've scarcely given her a thought. What a shit I've been.'

'Take it easy, Pen. Payback for that's what we're on about now.'

'I wonder why he killed her.'

'I think you'd have to say he has difficulty relating to women.'

I told her what Kelly had said about Bright's behaviour towards her and Melanie Kim. She shook her head and turned her attention to the material she'd printed out.

We worked through it for a couple of hours, drank wine and made notes. The politicians had standard careers— the ALP guy came from a union to a staff position with another MP until he got his slot. The National had a farming background and a degree in accounting. The Liberal had been a corporate lawyer who showed persistence by standing four times in elections and by-elections before winning his seat.

Their connections with businesses of one kind or another went back to their earliest years. Cartwright had been a go-between several times in disputes between waterside workers and stevedoring companies; Featherstone had worked for mining companies and sat on several of their boards; Polking-horn had been retained by a number of major companies and had successfully defended a big pharmaceutical firm in an action brought against them for marketing a dangerous product.

The researchers had uncovered existing connections—retainers not listed in declarations of interest, dodgy family trusts, family members in sinecures, favourable treatment by banks and credit-card companies, two DUI charges not proceeded with, an apprehended violence order violated but not followed up.

'Plenty of skeletons in those cupboards,' Pen said. 'Hard to say which is the most likely.'

I'd pushed the papers aside and was staring at the empty bottle.

'What? You reckon we should open another one?'

'No,' I said. 'Something just struck me. Bright really screwed up when he grabbed Kelly and killed Melanie Kim.'

'That's right.'

'He was working for someone then. He said he was. But would you keep him on after that? After he'd gone so far off the rails?'

'I suppose not. What're you saying?'

'Maybe he's not working for anyone now. Maybe he's gone freelance.'

17

'Makes it harder,' I said.

'Why?'

'Hard to guess what he'll do with the information. Would he sell it and, if so, who to? His former employer? Maybe, maybe not. Or perhaps he'd settle for blackmailing the pollies.'

Pen said, 'I hate the thought of him out there doing what he likes.'

'We don't know enough about him,' I said. 'This is going to be hard on you but you spent time with him in three phases, as it were—as the IT guy, as the heavy in Darwin, and later . . . travelling.'

'Delicately put.'

'Sorry. I said it wouldn't be easy. Try to remember everything you can about him—mannerisms, the things he said, what he ate, what he drank. What he watched on TV or showed an interest in. Anything that might help us get a handle on him. Can you do that?'

'I suppose. Rory spent almost as much time with him, more in Darwin.'

'That's true and I'm told he's left Darwin. Where would he go now that the Bright threat's lifted?'

'Home, I imagine, to lick his wounds. No, he put it on the market before we took off and he put all the furniture in storage.'

'Where else?'

'Friends, perhaps. But I don't know any of them.'

'Jack might have some idea.'

'Hold on. I remember that he had to see his surgeon for the last day of this month. I kept track of his appointments. That's the day after tomorrow. He was worried about missing it because he thought his leg wasn't coming along as well as it should.'

'Would he help us?'

'If there was something in it for him.'

She said O'Hara had been due to see his surgeon at 10.30 am at the Royal Prince Alfred Medical Centre in Camperdown.

We called it a day. We ate and watched TV. Pen tired quickly. She said she'd try to recollect everything she could about Bright after she'd had a sleep. I looked through the printout sheets and the notes we'd made without achieving any enlightenment. Of the politicians I disliked Polkinghorn the most because of his merchant bank connection and his defence of the pharmaceutical company. But that could just have been prejudice due to my resentment at the number of pills I had to take following my heart bypass.

As I was getting ready for bed I remembered what my chemist had said when I told him how boring taking the pills was. His reply was very like Wes Scott's.

'Be more boring out at Rookwood.'

I was smiling at that as I went to sleep. I woke up to feel the covers being raised and Pen slipping in beside me. She curled herself into my back.

'Just for the warmth and the company,' she said.

She'd left the bed when I woke up and I could hear Kasey Chambers's voice coming from below and smell coffee. I showered and dressed and found her in the kitchen drinking coffee and munching toast.

She waved her piece of toast. 'D'you usually sleep this late?'

'No, I usually get up at first light, do a hundred push-ups and jog five kilometres.'

'I doubt that, but you're in pretty good shape for an older guy.'

'Thanks. It was nice having you there last night.'

'Did me good. I'm not going to be one of those raped women who can't bear to look at or think of a man ever again.'

'Good.'

I had some breakfast and then we went up the street to get the papers and more coffee. She watched me swallow four pills.

'I'd like to collect my car,' she said. 'Have a bit of independence. Will you drive me to Bondi?'

'Sure. Independence? Do you want to find somewhere to stay?'

'Are you kicking me out?'

'Of course not.'

'Fine. I'm sticking with you until we see this thing through. I've been thinking about Bright and his habits. He has a slight accent. It's faint but it's there. Russian, at a guess. I know a bit about accents.'

I nodded. 'Anything else?'

'Don't jump up and down with excitement, will you? The only other thing is I saw him doing martial arts moves. You know—kicks and jumps. His hands . . . are very strong and hard.'

She was recovering a bit of the waspish part of her temperament but she was still quite vulnerable.

'That could be very useful,' I said.

'Don't . . . I was going to say don't patronise me. Sorry, I'm being a bitch this morning. Know why?'

I shook my head.

'I've usually had a drink by this time, maybe two. I'm going to try to cut it down. Do you think that's a good idea, Cliff?'

'It is, and it's bloody hard to do. Join the club.'

We drove to Bondi. She opened the garage and backed out a sporty VW Golf. We drove off, parked side by side down near the beach and walked along the concourse. There was a sharp wind; Pen wore a pea jacket I hadn't seen for years. It was too long in the sleeve for her and too wide in the shoulders but not by that much. She matched me stride for stride.

'Sorry to keep taking you back to it, but you said Bright drove to your lock-up in Bondi.'

'Yes. Why?'

'Did he know the way?'

'Oh, I see. Yes, like the back of his hand.'

Seeing the garage and knowing what had happened there brought up another question I'd been meaning to ask.

'Pen, why didn't you keep a copy, or copies?'

'Tried to. I transferred everything to Rory's computer to put it on a flash drive but the computer crashed and corrupted the stuff on Rory's machine. I didn't have another flash drive at the time so the data on my computer and the flash drive was all we had. I got caught up in all the arrangements for the tour and didn't do anything about it. I didn't think it was all that important just then. I didn't know Rory was going to talk about his plans. I used an iPad for the routine stuff.'

I could understand that. My backing up has always been erratic. I checked that Pen had her key and she went shopping for clothes. I drove to Newtown and visited Megan and Ben. Pen came back with bags and parcels and changed into fresh clothes and new shoes. We ate, and both drank less than we wanted to. We listened to some music and went to bed together. We lay with our arms around each other.

'Not yet,' she said.

'Okay.'

But it wasn't okay. I wanted her badly and it sharpened my determination to find Bright and see how he got on when he had more than terrified women and a drunk to deal with.

At ten-forty-five the next morning I was standing a little way along the corridor from the rooms of Dr Patrick Ross, orthopaedic surgeon, in the RPA Medical Centre. I'd been sitting in the coffee shop behind a newspaper since nine-thirty and had seen O'Hara arrive. He still looked puffy in the face, but he'd shaved and had his hair cut and styled in a way that at least partially concealed the retreating hairline.

He went to the X-ray unit as Pen had told me he would, and came out twenty-five minutes later carrying the X-rays in a bag. Then he caught the lift. At ten-fifteen I'd drifted past Dr Ross's glass door and seen Rory was the only patient waiting. He was gone by ten-thirty and I guessed his consultation wouldn't take more than thirty minutes. He'd seemed to be walking pretty easily without putting much weight on the stick. He wore a suit and tie, polished shoes.

At a little after eleven he came out looking pleased with

himself. He was carrying the stick rather than using it. I let him walk a few strides before stepping in front of him.

'Hello, Rory, X-rays good, were they?'

He stopped and his cheerful look fell away. 'Hardy. What the hell are you doing here?'

He lifted the stick as if to use it as a weapon but changed his mind.

'I'm here to ask for your help.'

He tried to brush past me. 'Not a chance.'

I crowded him against the wall. 'If you don't agree I'll break your other leg and you can go right back in and see Dr Ross.'

'You wouldn't.'

The corridor was empty. I grabbed him by the collar of his jacket and dragged him into the disabled toilet. I locked the door and wedged him between the toilet and washbasin with the support bar biting into his spine. I took his stick away and held him by the shoulders.

'Enough pressure this way and the right leg goes or maybe just the knee; the other way and you're back in rehab again for the left leg.'

'You're mad.'

I exerted some pressure and he yelped.

'I'm not mad, but I am angry.'

I pushed a little harder and he started to shake, which made it worse.

'Okay, okay, whatever you say. What do you want?'

'A couple of things. You're going to come with me. We'll meet up with Penelope and we'll take it from there. You remember her, don't you?'

I released him and he drew in a deep breath. 'Of course I do.'

'Worried about her, were you?'

'I'm worried about every fucking thing. I don't know what I'm doing.'

'Well, here's a chance for you to do something useful.'

I shepherded him out of the building and across to where I'd parked. He offered no resistance. He'd arrived by cab. He said he hadn't driven since his accident and that he'd lost his nerve for driving in Sydney's traffic. All of a sudden he seemed to need his stick again for support.

He was silent on the short drive to Glebe except to ask what had happened to Pen and how she was. I told him I'd let her answer that. He noticed the Golf parked outside my place. We went into the house and through to the living room where Pen was sitting in a chair, turning the pages of the *Sydney Morning Herald*. O'Hara stopped in his tracks and Pen let the paper slide from her lap to the floor. They exchanged the look of lovers when the thrill is gone.

'You two have a chat,' I said. 'I've got some calls to make.'

I went upstairs and hung around for a few minutes. Their voices were low at first but rose as the talk became heated and some bitter things started to be said.

I came down to find O'Hara sitting on the couch

massaging his leg. Pen had picked up the paper and laid it aside. She was staring, stone-faced, at the bank of CDs and DVDs. I knew that she wanted a drink. I winked at her.

'Let's have a drink,' I said.

I went to the kitchen, opened a bottle of red and poured three glasses. I left the bottle in the kitchen and put the glasses on the coffee table. I sat in a chair opposite Pen, who picked up her glass and took a small sip. O'Hara drank his off in a gulp and seemed to regain a bit of his spirit.

'You're fucking this gorilla, are you?'

'Not yet,' Pen said.

'This is how I see it,' I said. 'There've been some casualties since you started playing your tricky games. You're one yourself, with the leg, and there's the IT guy Bright nobbled; but Melanie Kim's dead, Kelly's got a serious coke problem and now you know what happened to Pen. I reckon you have some responsibility here.'

O'Hara fiddled with his empty glass. 'You could say that. Are you appealing to my better nature?'

'I think you've probably got one somewhere, but you're a mess and you'll stay that way until this is cleared up.'

'Cleared up how?'

'By putting Bright out of action and reclaiming all that dirt and data you gathered and . . . decommissioning it. Then you'd have a clean slate and could start putting your life back together again. You've got talents.'

'Can I have another drink?'

'We're going slow, Pen and me. You could do the same.'

'Shit, you're a moralistic bastard.'

'He's just applying the pressure, Rory,' Pen said. 'You used to say you were good at handling pressure.'

'I thought I was. I'm not so sure now.'

'Let's start off easy,' I said. 'When I asked Pen to tell me everything she could about Bright, one of the things was that he went through some martial arts exercises. That's all we have apart from knowing he's left-handed and has a slight accent.'

'Hapkido.'

'What?'

'It's a Korean martial arts style. I was chatting to Bright before all this shit happened, about the only time I talked to him then, and I just mentioned that I'd done karate when I was younger. Can't remember why. Anyway, he virtually sneered at me and said it was for wimps and that he did this hapkido. I looked it up—it's very violent, so violent the people doing it have to be well padded to avoid crippling each other.'

I looked at Pen. 'A Russian who practises hapkido. Can't be too many places around that cater to that stuff.'

'So I've been helpful,' O'Hara said and he held up his glass.

I took it out to the kitchen and refilled it. They didn't speak to each other while I was gone.

'Yeah, that was helpful,' I said. 'But there's more you can do.'

'Shit, what else?'

'I want you standing by. If I can't find Bright with the information we've got, you're going to help me flush him out.'

'Why would I do that?'

'Because if you do I'll help you to become a celebrity all over again.'

'How?'

'Wait and see.'

18

O'Hara was staying with a friend in Haberfield. He gave us the address, the landline and his mobile number. I called him a cab and he left, summoning up some reserves of dignity.

'How are you going to make him a celebrity again?' Pen said.

'I don't know.'

'You were bluffing? That's devious; you might even say ruthless. He's in a pretty bad way.'

'Maybe, but I wanted to keep him on tap and that seemed the best way to do it. What was the verbal stoush about?'

'He was trying to persuade me to come back to him.'

'You can't do that. I've got work for you to do.'

She laughed. 'You,' she said. 'Okay, what work?'

I told her that we'd have to try to find all the places in Sydney where hapkido was taught or practised.

'Can't be many, from the sound of it,' she said. 'Web job. You can do that.'

'Right. And then we have to go to those places to see if Bright is on their books. You'll have to do the asking.'

'Why?'

'They're more likely to respond to a woman than a man, especially a good-looking one. Did you buy any . . . fancy clothes?'

'D'you mean sexy?'

'I suppose I do.'

'Not really.'

'You'd better get some. You'll have to be disguised in case Bright is actually on the spot. You'll need a wig.'

Her bruises were fading but still visible. She touched her face.

'Heavy makeup,' I said. 'More disguise.'

She said she knew where to buy a wig and went off to do it. I got on the web and searched for hapkido in Sydney, coming up with only three gyms—in Crows Nest, Stanmore and Auburn. I wrote down the addresses and waited for Pen to come back. She walked in wearing a black wig and dark glasses that transformed her. She laughed at my reaction.

'Wait till I get dressed,' she said.

'Look, there's no rush. It's lunchtime.'

'Fuck lunch. Let's get going.'

She hadn't quite finished the wine from before. I drank it.

After what seemed like an hour but probably wasn't, she came down the stairs, treading slowly and carefully. She reached the bottom, pirouetted and posed. She wore a tight, low-cut print top under a skimpy, shiny leather jacket; an impossibly short black skirt, black tights and stilettos. The black hair was a wild riot of shapes and her makeup was bold. She fluttered false eyelashes.

'Too tarty?' she said.

I cleared my throat. 'No, just right.'

'Where are we going?'

I showed her the list. 'You choose.'

'Crows Nest.'

I'd put the .38 in the pocket of my leather jacket while she was away. I pulled the jacket on and we went out and got into the Golf. Pen handled the car well despite the wrist injury and seemed to enjoy herself. She parked in Alexander Street opposite the gym, which, like most of them, featured big windows and glass doors. Pen giggled when she saw me put on a baseball cap and a scarf that I allowed to ride up to cover the lower part of my face.

'It's odds against him actually being there,' I said. 'But I'll hang as close as I can.'

'What do I do?'

'You're his girlfriend. You describe him minutely and say you're sorry for breaking up with him and you desperately want him back. You don't know where he is. All you know is that he's a hapkido fanatic.'

'I'm distressed, right?'

'Very.'

We crossed the street, Pen tottering on the very high heels. Inside the glass doors was a lobby with the gym on one side and a physiotherapy business on the other. There were pamphlets on a stand outside the physio place; I took one and pretended to study it while getting as close as I could to the gym door. I saw Pen approach the desk where a man with broad shoulders and a shaven head was tapping at a computer. He looked up as Pen spoke and seemed glad to be interrupted.

Pen was animated. She got as close to the man as she could and put her hand on his arm. She pushed back the sleeves of her jacket and top, showing him the cast on her wrist. He was all sympathy but he shook his head. Pen let her shoulders slump as she walked away. His eyes followed her to the door.

I went across the road and waited by the car.

'No dice,' she said.

'Better luck next time. You played it perfectly.'

We repeated the process at Stanmore and Auburn with the same result. Pen was tired and disappointed and I drove us back to Glebe.

'You don't seem cast down,' she said.

'I'd have been surprised if it'd worked. It's never that easy. We'll just have to think of another angle.'

She sat back and closed her eyes. I tried not to look too often at her long slender legs in the tights and the way the skirt had ridden up almost to her crotch.

Back at the house she changed into the clothes she'd worn before but kept the wig and the makeup on—'For fun,' she said. We ordered a delivery of Thai food and I opened a bottle of white wine.

'Second drink and it's after seven o' clock,' she said. 'That's a first.'

She tried to remember anything else significant about Bright but came up empty. I told her not to worry.

'We might tackle it from the politicians' end,' I said.

'How?'

'Have to think.'

We watched the news on television and Woody Allen's *Midnight in Paris*, which put us both in a good mood. We said goodnight and went upstairs. I switched on the reading lamp and went to bed with the Dormandy book on opium. The door opened and Pen came in. She was still wearing the makeup and wig but she was barefoot and dressed in only a lacy black slip. She slid into the bed and kissed me.

'Be gentle,' she said, 'be very gentle.'

I was.

19

We made love again in the morning and lay in the tangled bedclothes. Pen suddenly rolled away.

'Canberra,' she said.

'What?'

'I've just remembered that the guy in Stanmore said there was a hapkido place in Canberra. Wouldn't it make sense for Bright to be in Canberra if he's been caught up with lobbyists and he has plans to blackmail politicians?'

'Yeah, maybe.'

'There are lots of Russians in Canberra—at the universities, the embassy.'

'At the Institute of Sport.'

'You're making fun of me.'

'Yes, but it's not a bad idea. Better than anything I've come up with.'

'You were talking about coming at it from the politicians' angle.'

'Right. I haven't had any bright ideas along those lines but we could think about it some more. Yes, why not?'

We got out of bed. Pen shivered in her slip.

'Colder in Canberra,' I said.

'Calls for some faux fur and boots.'

Quick showers and warm clothes. Pen found the Ainslie Gym in the suburb of that name and I booked us online into the Northbourne Motel. We were on the road in the Falcon soon after 10 am.

'Sure this'll get us there?' Pen said.

'It's got me pretty well everywhere I've needed to go for a good few years. More room for your long legs and I'm on expenses. Neville Kim can pay for the petrol.'

'And the motel?'

'Yup.'

'Meals, drinks?'

'I exercise my judgement.'

'Will you tell him about me?'

'There are some things a client doesn't need to know.'

We made good time on the freeway and after a stop for fresh air and coffee at the halfway point, we were in Canberra before one-thirty. I checked us in as Hardy and Smith. As usual, the room wouldn't be ready until mid-afternoon. We left our bags and Pen walked down to the CBD to do some shopping. I took a long aimless walk to get rid of the driving stiffness. The day was clear and still but the air was bitingly cold and, despite a coat, gloves and a scarf, I had to walk briskly to keep warm.

When I got back Pen was in the bathroom, wearing her wig and putting on her makeup. She wore the clothes she'd had on the day before plus a pair of spike-heeled shiny black boots. A silk-lined silvery jacket with fake fur collar and cuffs lay on the bed. She came out, slipped the jacket on and posed.

'How's this?'

'Terrific.' I opened the mini-bar. 'Time for a bracer against the cold. What's your fancy?'

'Did you know,' Pen said as we drove towards Ainslie, an inner suburb of Canberra, 'that the White Australia policy had a bit to do with the choice of Canberra for a capital?'

'No. How was that?'

'I read about it somewhere. The thinking at the time was that white people were creative because they lived in cold climates. They avoided the hot-climate torpor of the coloureds, so the capital of a new white man's country should be in a cold place.'

'Well, it's certainly cold, but I wouldn't say Canberra's an advertisement for creativity and productivity. Think of the parliament.'

The gym was on the second level of a three-storey building in Ainslie's small shopping precinct. Mount Ainslie, just a big hill, rose up behind it. As before, Pen went in, all long legs and fluttering eyes. I was able to watch her performance from the stairs leading up to the top level. I told myself Bright was unlikely to recognise her even if he was there, but it could get sticky.

Pen went through her routine with the guy at the desk and he nodded affirmatively. Pen persisted but he shook his head. She favoured him with a high candlepower smile and walked out.

I came down the stairs and took her arm. 'Success?'

'Yes, he comes here. He uses the name Steve Ball. I tried to get him to give me his address or a phone number but he wouldn't.'

'So we'll just have to watch the place.'

'Not exactly. He said Steve's due in for a sparring session at four o'clock this afternoon. That's only an hour from now.'

'I'm looking forward to seeing him in action.'

'And then what?'

'Follow him home, I guess, and think about it.'

We waited in the car park the clients used to access the gym from a back entrance. I turned the engine on to run the heater from time to time. Pen was quiet, plucking loose threads from her jacket. I noticed that she'd added false fingernails to her outfit, painted silver to match her jacket.

'How will you feel when you see him?' I asked.

'I'll feel like kicking him in the balls, but I won't.'

Four o'clock came and went and there was no sign of

Bright. We went up to the gym and I could hear heavy thumps and loud, hissing breathing. Pen looked disappointed and upset, which gave me an idea.

'Idiots,' she said, looking at the padded, leaping men.

'Can you cry?'

'What?'

'Can you cry, or look as if you've been crying?'

'I can't just cry, but I could smear this mascara, I suppose.'

'Do it. Go in and work on him. You're terribly disappointed and upset.'

'I am.'

'Try to get something more out of him, anything.'

She took a tissue from her shoulder bag, wet it with saliva and dabbed at her eyes. The mascara left smudges near her cheekbones. She pulled her top down to reveal more cleavage and tottered inside. I took up my former position and watched as she pleaded with the man at the desk.

She dug for tissues in her bag. Her shoulders shook and she threw back her head several times and almost lost her balance. He put out his hand to steady her and she clasped it. He resisted, but only briefly.

She came out looking quite dishevelled with her face stained, the heavy lipstick smeared, and the jacket slipping off one shoulder.

On the stairs going down I straightened the jacket. 'How did it go?'

'I did cry.'

'I thought you might.'
'He said he didn't have a phone number and all he'd tell me was that Steve lived in a place called Gundaroo.'

20

I didn't know the southern tablelands area well so I looked Gundaroo up on my laptop. It was in New South Wales but close to Canberra—only about a half-hour's drive away. It was described as a village, with agriculture as its main activity. Academics and public servants from Canberra had weekenders there and small blocks for hobby farms and keeping horses. It was a tourist attraction for its heritage quality.

I absorbed this while Pen got out of her fuck-me outfit, as Germaine Greer might have called it. She took her time about it and when she'd finished it was far too late to do any hunting.

I phoned Neville Kim and told him what I was doing, although not that I'd narrowed the search down as far as I had.

'That's very encouraging,' he said. 'I have some friends in Canberra. I'll give you a couple of phone numbers to use should you need help.'

I wrote them down and promised to keep him informed. Pen stuffed the glamour gear into a plastic shopping bag.

'Might keep the boots,' she said.

'Why not?'

She asked who I'd been talking to and I told her about Kim's offer of help.

'Will we need help?'

'I'm trying not to get ahead of myself. I'm already out on a limb. By rights, a private detective should check in with the police, especially when there's a wanted criminal involved.'

'Are you going to do that?'

'Not just now. Maybe when we locate him.'

We drove into Civic and ate at a Spanish restaurant. We both had garlic prawns and garlic chicken. I had a beer and we shared a small carafe of white wine. The restaurant was half full on a weeknight.

Over coffee Pen said, 'Are you going to charge it to your client?'

I reached for her hand. 'No, this is just about you and me.'

We'd left the air-conditioning on high in the motel. We stripped off, made love and ended up slick with the motel's scented oil and damp with perspiration.

We drove to Gundaroo in the morning. I had the photograph of Bright, which Neville Kim had rightly described as blurry, my PIA licence and my experience to work with. Asking the right questions to find someone was my bread and butter and I set about it. Pen had insisted on coming along although there was nothing for her to do. She bought newspapers and magazines and installed herself in a coffee shop.

The heritage buildings, and the tendency of people to greet each other in the street more than they do in the city, gave the place its village air. Showing the photograph and my licence and downplaying the seriousness of the matter, I inquired in a few of the obvious places—service station, general store, newsagent—without success.

I sat with Pen and had a coffee. The coffee and croissant culture had reached Gundaroo, as it had most small places with any claims to olde-worlde atmosphere.

'No luck?'

'So far. Tell me, did Bright drink in Darwin?'

She considered. 'Not much.'

'What did he drink?'

'Beer.'

The Heritage Inn had undergone renovations over time to make it comfortable for twenty-first century` drinkers but it retained the original nineteenth-century structure and a big effort had been made to preserve the historical features. I went into the bar, ordered a middy of Carlton Black and dropped my change in the tips glass. I drank, waited until the barman had served another of the half-dozen customers, and went through my routine.

'Lousy picture,' he said.

'Yes.'

'What's he done?'

It was the first bite I'd had.

'Nothing, as far as I know. He's a friend of someone else I'm looking for who might have done something, if you see what I mean.'

'Yeah, well looks like Steve Ball. Bit skinnier than that, though. Comes in occasionally. No trouble.'

'That's good. Do you happen to know where he lives?'

'He's got a place out Gundaroo Road north about five klicks. Old joint on a couple of acres, bit tumbledown. Been there for the last few years, off and on.'

He moved away to serve another customer. I finished my beer, turned to go, and asked casually, 'What does he drive?'

The barman scratched his head. 'Seen it once. A Jeep, I think. Yeah, a blue Jeep.'

I thanked him again and left. Pen was looking bored when I rejoined her but she sparked up at the news.

'Let's go,' she said.

'Okay, but this is simply surveillance. Then we go back to Canberra and you stay there.'

'While you do what?'

'Call the police in.'

'And arrest him. I'd like to see that.'

'No.'

'Why not?'

'Cops and guns—it wouldn't be safe.'

I followed the barman's instructions, keeping an eye on the odometer. It was seven kilometres rather than five, but country people always underestimate distance. The blocks showed signs of being cared for—good fences and gates, strategically placed stands of trees, graded, well-drained tracks. A few of the cottages were visible from the road and looked presentable.

Bright's place was easy to spot. It let the side down badly; the rusty gate sagged on its hinges and the fence had gaps, partly repaired by star stakes and wire. I drove by slowly. The track was muddy and rutted and led to a garage that would have offered minimal protection. No sign of a car.

'He's not there,' Pen said.

'But he could be close by. We can't hang around here. I just want to scout a bit up there where the road bends.'

'Why?'

'Looks to be a track running beside his property and quite a few trees. We'll need some cover while we prepare.'

I drove up to the bend, which put me the best part of a hundred metres from Bright's gate. A patch of thick bush started there and the track appeared to be a fire trail into the forest. I got some binoculars from the glove box and told Pen to stay put.

The drive had been uphill and it was colder out here than back in the town. I pulled up the hood on my anorak and walked into the bush. I was lifting the binoculars when I heard a faint sound behind me. I felt a blow to the side of my head that stunned me. Then another blow to the same place and the ground tilted and a big gum tree came rushing to meet me.

21

I came out of it in a room I didn't recognise and in the company of three men I didn't know. One wore a suit and a professional air, the other two wore casual clothes—jeans, bomber jackets, sneakers—and if they were professionals it was at something different from the man in the suit. I was sitting on a chair; a plastic restraint anchored my right wrist to the armrest. My anorak was hanging on the back of the chair.

'I'm a doctor, Mr Hardy,' the suit said as he bent over me. 'Do you know what day it is?'

'Yes.'

'And the date?'

I told him the date.

'You've been concussed, but not too badly. The hood you were wearing softened the blow.'

I looked at the two others. 'Blows,' I said.

The doctor nodded. 'Yes, bruises and some abrasions from where you hit the tree. How's your vision?'

'Okay.'

'Hearing?'

'A bit of ringing.'

'Normal.'

'Where's Penelope?'

'She's safe.'

'That doesn't answer the question.'

The doctor moved away.

'It's all the answer you'll get,' one of the others said.

'Who're you two?'

The stocky one was doing the talking; the taller one was the strong silent type.

'You could call me Mr A and him Mr B.'

'That'd be A for arsehole and B for bastard.'

'I should've hit you harder,' B said.

'Maybe you should have. What's this all about?'

'Just be patient,' A said. 'Someone'll be here soon to speak to you.'

In a situation like that there's an impulse to talk out of nervousness. It's best to suppress it. The room was small and neat with a single bed, the chair I was sitting on and not much else. A and B stood over by the door, A with his arms folded, B with big hands dangling. Through the window I could see foliage of some kind. I looked at my watch but the glass had cracked and it had stopped. I had no way of knowing how long I'd been unconscious.

The two men looked capable and I was tied to a chair. In the movies I'd have been able to swing the chair and flatten them both. Or use my cigarette lighter to melt the plastic restraint. But the chair was fairly heavy and I didn't have a cigarette lighter. I was worried about Pen but I'd been told she was safe and I hadn't been damaged other than in the initial attack. Something was brewing, disagreeable most likely, but probably not life-threatening.

'What's the time?'

A looked at his watch, then he grinned. 'What do you care? It's afternoon.'

'I could do with some water.'

'Get him a glass of water,' A said.

That confirmed the hierarchy. B went out, leaving the door open. I was pretty sure I could hear traffic, so I wasn't out in the bush and it wasn't a big house. A kicked the door shut.

'Why did you do that?'

No answer.

'She's in the house, isn't she?'

The flicker of annoyance crossing his face told me I was right. B came back and handed me the water in a plastic cup—light as a feather, useless. I drank it and flipped the cup at him. He fumbled the catch and swore.

The door opened and a man walked in carrying a chair. He set it down about a metre away from me and jerked his head at A and B. They left and the newcomer took his seat after carefully gauging the distance between us and moving the chair back half a metre.

He was medium-sized, dark, with short hair and heavy stubble. He wore a well-cut grey suit and the slight bulge under the jacket on the left said holstered gun.

'How's the head?'

'Not too bad. Are you going to tell me what's going on here? Where's Penelope?'

'She's here, undamaged.'

'Better be.'

'You're not really in a position to say something like that, are you?'

I didn't answer.

He rubbed the bristles on his face, already sprouting so early in the day. 'You can call me Jones.'

'All right, Jones, what's going on?'

'Let's get things straight at your end. You're a private detective working for Melanie Kim's brother to deal with the man known sometimes as Sean Bright. You located him through some pretty smart detective work and were just getting the lay of the land when you became careless.'

'She told you all that?'

'She did.'

'What did you do to her?'

'Nothing, I told you. It seems she cares about you. She told me because I said I'd kill you if she didn't. That's all it took.'

He was sitting very still, not fidgeting, a serious man.

'What are you?'

'If I told you I was a member of the Federal Police would you believe me?'

'No.'

'What if I told you I used to be in the Federal Police and now I do similar work in a private ... no, a corporate capacity.'

He was trying to induce me to say yes. It was a standard bonding technique—start small with yes and work up. I said nothing.

'Ms Milton-Smith says you intended to have the police arrest Bright.'

'That was one of the options.'

'Yes, you have something of a vigilante reputation, but I'm inclined to think that's what you'd have done. I'm afraid I can't allow that to happen.'

'How would you stop me?'

'Very simply, by holding Ms Milton-Smith to ensure your compliance.' He flipped his hand over. 'The other side of the coin, you see—her concern for you, your concern for her.'

'Why?'

'Bright has been foolish enough to attempt to blackmail several people. One of those people was foolish enough to try to enlist our help. But we're more concerned with what Bright is blackmailing this person *about*, rather than protecting him.'

'So, why don't you just grab Bright and get hold of the information he has? Then let him take the consequences. He's a murderer—and a rapist, by the way.'

'That's deplorable, but it's not so simple. You see Bright has an accomplice and he's threatened that if any action is taken against him, his accomplice releases all the information to the media and the authorities. You can see how that would not be in our interest.'

If Jones had been a Federal cop it must have been at a high level. Everything about him bespoke intelligence, experience and success. It was a powerful combination, adding up to a persuasive and compelling personality. I struggled to keep my mental distance from him.

'I can see how you've got yourself in a bind.'

'For the moment, yes. But we're working on finding out who the accomplice is. We have massive surveillance on Bright, physical, electronic, the works. That's why you couldn't be allowed to blunder in.'

I started thinking about candidates for Bright's accomplice.

'Pondering?' Jones said. 'Haven't I made myself clear?'

'Tell me, when did your . . . organisation start to take an interest in this? Does it have a name, by the way?'

'Various names that need not concern you. We became involved when Rory O'Hara made his announcement about politicians being interested in joining his new party. We'd already targeted this individual I've referred to and thought it likely he was among them.'

'You must have been alarmed when Bright killed the Korean woman.'

'Not particularly. Unpleasant things happen when big money and big projects are at stake. A good many things deemed accidents are actually not, as you probably know.'

'Hence your threat to kill me.'

'A threat is just words, but yes, if need be. I've said all I have to say to you, Hardy. If you're hoping to talk your way out of this, you're mistaken.'

I straightened up in the chair and spoke with more confidence than I felt. 'I think I might be able to help you find the accomplice. My involvement goes back further and deeper than yours.'

He rubbed his bristles again, his wedding ring scraping against the stubble. 'I think you're bluffing.'

'I'm not bluffing. I've got a shrewd idea I know the person you want. And I think you're at a stalemate. You need a breakthrough, Mr Jones.'

He sighed. 'Of course you'd impose conditions.'

'Quite a few, yes.'

'Such as?'

'You give me free rein to go back to Sydney to find the man I'm thinking of. No supervision.'

'If I agree to that, you'd see that I'd have to keep the woman.'

'Yes, but you'd have to allow me to talk to her first and guarantee her safety and comfort.'

He nodded. 'What else?'

'If it all works out and you get the information you want or confirm that it doesn't exist, that neutralises Bright, correct?'

'Yes.'

'Then you help me to arrange his arrest for the murder of Melanie Kim.'

'That could be a pleasure. Give me a minute to think about this.'

His thinking involved a fair bit of stubble-stroking and gazing out the window. He took out a packet of cigarettes and offered it to me. I shook my head. He lit his cigarette with a lighter and took a deep drag.

'As I said, I know something of your reputation. I talked to some of my former colleagues in the Federal Police. I believe you've had dealings with them?'

'Once or twice.'

'They dislike you of course, but they admit that you are persistent and see things through.'

'I'm like a dog with a bone.'

'I'm inclined to take a chance on you.'

'Won't you need to consult a higher power?'

'Now you're being offensive.' He went to the door and spoke quietly to someone, A and B entered the room and B used a Swiss Army knife to cut the plastic restraint. He nicked my wrist and it bled a little.

'We'll put Ms Milton-Smith in the picture,' Jones said. 'All three of us are armed, so no heroics.'

* * *

The hardest thing then was reconciling Pen to the arrangement and I didn't succeed. The room where she was held was considerably more comfortable than the one I'd been in, bigger, with a double bed, a closet, a desk and chair and an ensuite. Pen was sitting in an armchair looking furious when we trooped in.

'What's going on, Cliff? Who are these bastards?'

Jones gestured for B to leave. A leaned against the door, Jones sat at the desk, I sat on the bed and explained the circumstances to Pen. She kept interrupting and shaking her head.

'You have no choice, Ms Milton-Smith,' Jones said.

'Marinos,' Pen said. 'I've decided to go back to my real name. Deprivation of liberty is a serious crime. How long d'you plan to keep it up?'

'Well, that's an important question,' Jones said. 'How long, Hardy?'

'A week.'

'Four days.'

'Who is this accomplice you're both on about?'

'I can't tell you, Pen.'

The look she gave me was icy and her tone was detached, clinical. 'Your forehead and your wrist are bleeding.'

'He'll be patched up,' Jones said. 'That's all. Hardy, your time starts now.'

22

The doctor cleaned the cuts and applied some antiseptic and bandaids. Jones handed me my anorak and a slip of paper with two mobile phone numbers written on it.

'Your gun's in the glove box of your car and the bullets are in the pocket of your jacket. You'll phone me when you have something to report.'

'Suppose I don't have anything to report?'

'Then I think it unlikely you'll ever see Ms ... Marinos again.'

We were standing, Jones, A and B and me, on the porch of a suburban house sheltered from the road by a high hedge. I'd heard voices at the back of the house, so Pen hadn't been left unguarded.

'No harm in you seeing where we are,' Jones said, 'because we won't be here long.'

'Do you guarantee she'll be kept somewhere at least as comfortable as where she is now?'

'Better. These blokes will accompany you in your car back to your motel. You'll give them Ms Marinos's clothing and personal effects.'

Jones went back into the house. A jabbed me in the ribs with a pistol, B twisted my arm up behind my back and we walked to a carport where the Falcon stood.

'In the back,' A said.

I climbed in with him following me. B got behind the wheel.

'I hope you can drive a manual,' I said.

B started the engine, had trouble finding reverse and kangaroo-hopped.

'Thought not. Takes an honest man to drive an old Falcon.'

'Shut up,' A said.

B tried again, stalled and swore.

'Can't catch, can't drive,' I said. 'What good is he?'

B turned around, his face a mask of fury. A told him to calm down and get the hang of driving the manual. After a few false starts he had the car moving and managed a few grating gear changes.

'He's stuffing my gearbox.'

'I told you to shut up. Just concentrate on what you have to do to prevent you and the woman ending up dead.'

A sign told me the suburb was Scullin. The Belconnen Way took us back to the city. The driver had an aggressive style and once he'd got the feel of the car he enjoyed going full pelt and changing lanes.

'Handles well,' he said.

'Who cares?' A said.

We pulled up outside the room and A produced the key as we got out of the car. They herded me to the door, which A unlocked.

'After you,' he said.

We went in. The room had been cleaned and made neat. I packed Pen's clothes into the overnight bag. The spike-heeled boots wouldn't fit.

A pointed to the big shopping bag that held her dress-up items. 'What about that?'

'She won't want it.'

B emptied the contents onto the bed and whistled. He picked up the boots.

'You're a lucky man,' he said. 'I'd like to see her in this gear.'

That was just enough distraction. I took one step and hit him as hard as I could just above the belt buckle. The wind went out of him in a rush and he bent double. I thumped his forehead with the heel of my hand and he collapsed to the floor.

'Now we're even,' I said.

I turned to A. 'Give me the room key and the car keys, pick him up and the two of you can piss off.'

A didn't speak. He helped B, still gasping for breath, to his feet, reached into B's pocket and got the car keys. He threw them and the motel key on the bed. I handed him the bag with Pen's things in it. He helped B to the door where he turned and gave me a hard stare.

'We'll see you again, Hardy.'

'I hope so. Tell your mate not to be ashamed. I just did to him what Fitzsimmons did to Corbett. Legitimate blow.'

'You're mad.'

'Do you mean insane or angry? Maybe I'm both.'

He shook his head and they left, B limping and swearing and A abusing him. I shut the door and opened the mini-bar.

Half an hour later, with some scotch and paracetamol inside me, packed and checked out, I was on the road to Sydney. Pen's sexy outfit was in a wheelie bin at the motel and her boots were on the back seat. Her last expression stayed with me until well back inside New South Wales.

My target was Gordon Glassop. I remembered how nervous he was when I'd questioned him in the bus on the way back from Wollongong. At the time I'd put it down to the events of the night before and his innate wimpiness. I remembered Kelly saying that Glassop had splashed money around. I'd thought it was money O'Hara and Pen had paid him for documents, but O'Hara had said that wasn't much. And how did Bright know to go to Darwin after them? It looked to me as if Glassop was cooperating with Bright, probably not willingly. Bright was a scary character, but given the way I was feeling, so was I.

Pen obviously knew how to contact Glassop but I couldn't afford to mention his name in front of Jones and co. When I reached the city I pulled over and rang the mobile number O'Hara had given me.

'This is Rory.'

'This is Hardy.'

'Hardy. Jesus Christ, what do you want?'

'Do you know where Gordon Glassop lives?'

'Why?'

'Just answer the question.'

'The answer is no and if I did know I wouldn't tell you where he is because you'd tell him where I am and I owe him money.'

'Who would know?'

'Pen.'

I didn't respond. There was a pause and then a triumphant tone entered his voice.

'She's not with you. Well, well, didn't work out, eh?'

I hung up. Kelly had said that Glassop had tried to get her to fuck him and she'd played along far enough to be able to borrow money from him. Had she played along as far as his place?

It was after 6 pm and I was tired, but four days isn't long to find someone. I drove to Riley Street in Surry Hills, parked illegally and rang the bell at Kelly's house.

The woman who answered was blonde and dressed not unlike the way Pen had in her siren role.

'You're early,' she said.

'I'm not your client, darling. I'm looking for Kelly Scott.'

She heaved a theatrical sigh, her heavy breasts rose. 'Cop?'

'Sort of.'

'She's in the pub. Fuck off.'

I used the same ATM as before and drew out $500. There were smokers on the footpath outside the pub and inside it was dark, crowded and noisy with a combination of music, poker machines and conversation. I worked my way to the bar, bought a beer, and began to move between the tables and the clusters of standing drinkers. Eventually I located Kelly at a table in a group of four, two men and two women.

Kelly was drunk. I could hear her voice above the din as she abused one of the men. She was waving her glass around, threatening to spill whatever was in it on people standing nearby. The other woman in the group was pawing at Kelly and the other man was looking annoyed. He grabbed the woman, pulled her off her chair and dragged her away. Kelly drained her glass and handed it to the remaining man. He shook his head and walked away. Kelly slumped against the wall, fumbling in her bag.

'Hello, Kel,' I said. 'How's it going?'

She squinted at me blearily. Her hair was greasy and tangled and her heavy eye-makeup was smudged; her silk dress was stained and her jacket was ash-smeared.

'It's non-fucking Cliff Hardy. Changed your mind, Cliffy? Looking for a root?'

'No, for information, like before.'

'Infor-fucking-mation, that's all you care about. Buy me a drink.'

'You've had enough. I saw the barman looking at you. I don't think he'd serve me one for you. You're close to being chucked out.'

'Who gives a shit?' She took a packet of cigarettes from her bag.

'You can't smoke in here. Come outside. We'll find somewhere you can smoke and have some coffee. I'll make it worth your while.'

'My while ain't worth much. Hey, that's a joke.'

Tears appeared in her eyes. She was close to breaking down. I put my arm around her, eased her off the chair, hooked her bag over her shoulder and guided her to the door. She staggered when the cold air hit her. I held her while she stumbled to the gutter and vomited convulsively. One of the smokers laughed, then cut the laugh off short when I looked at him.

I straightened her up and gave her a tissue to wipe her mouth. She leaned against me and began to cry.

'Come on, take some deep breaths.'

'Jesus, I'm a mess.'

'Temporarily,' I said.

I steered her down the street to a coffee bar with tables on the footpath. I sat her down. A waiter came out and looked at us dubiously—a dishevelled woman and a man with sticking plaster on his forehead and, to judge from the reaction I'd just had, a very threatening look.

I showed him a $20 note. 'Water, and two long blacks.'

Kelly sat with her head bowed. The waiter came back with a carafe of water and two glasses. I fished in Kelly's bag, found a pocket packet of tissues and wet several. I put them on the table in front of her.

'Clean yourself up. You'll feel better.'

Without lifting her head, she used the tissues. The coffee arrived. I took her cigarettes from her bag and passed them to her. Still not looking at me, she shook her head. I poured her some water and she drank it.

Slowly, her head came up. With the makeup wiped and the tears blotted she looked like a damaged Barbie doll.

'Like I said, I'm a mess.'

'We all have our bad patches.'

'This is one for sure. Thanks for your help back there. Christ, I'm drunk and coked with it. What do you want, Hardy?'

'It can wait. Drink some coffee.'

'Coffee, ugh,' she said, but she drank, using both hands on the cup.

I sipped my long black. It was scalding hot but she drank hers in a couple of gulps without seeming to notice.

'More,' she said.

I pushed my cup across. She dumped four spoonfuls of sugar into it and drank it fast.

'That's more sugar than I would have had in five years when I was a model.'

I nodded. She picked up the cigarettes, got her lighter from the bag and lit up.

'And I lived on these. It's not a healthy lifestyle and it's not that much fun.'

'Money's good, though.'

She took a couple of deep drags. 'Not that good, after managers, agents, pills. Christ, the pills I took. Okay, you've got me up and running. What do you want and how much can you pay?'

I'd thought through what I should tell her and I kept to the script. I said I needed to talk to Glassop to learn more about Bright.

'Bloody different characters,' she said. 'I don't reckon they related to each other much.'

'Right, but you know what those IT nerds are like. They spy on each other.'

'Do they?'

'So I'm told. Now you said when you met Glassop in the wine bar he was trying to get off with you.'

'Don't remind me. That lip-licking, ugh.'

'Did you go home with him?'

'Let's talk money.'

'You did, didn't you?'

'Yeah, all I wanted from him was the same as what I want from you and that's money. But in your case I wouldn't mind so much if I had to fuck you to get it.'

'Thanks a lot. You know the address?'

'Of course I know it. He was too pissed to drive, so I had to drive his crappy Honda.'

'What happened to the acting job?'

'I didn't get it.'

'What're you doing now?'

'Three fucking guesses.'

I fished the $500 out of my pocket. Her eyes didn't light up. She stubbed out her cigarette and lit another. 'Have you seen Rory and Penelope?'

'Yes.'

'How are they?'

'Not together.'

She smiled and reached for the money. 'Nineteen Scott Street. Hard to forget. My name and I was nineteen once.'

'Where?'

'Shitty little place in Balmain.'

'Phone number?'

'Are you kidding?'

23

The concussion, the encounter with Jones, the drive to Sydney and the session with Kelly were enough for one day. I drove home, ate a sandwich, drank some wine, took some painkillers and fell into bed with my mobile alarm set for 6 am. Pen's scent was on the pillows and sheets and her black slip was lying across the bed. It suggested that she wanted to come back, which was exactly what I wanted.

In the morning I showered and shaved and decided I could get by with another flesh-coloured band-aid on the forehead scrape. I'm a quick healer; the cut on my wrist had scabbed. By seven-twenty I was outside number 19 Scott Street, a narrow, single-storey terrace. Like a few other places in the street, the kerb was interrupted by a driveway and the area in the front of the house had been disfigured by a carport. A Honda Civic nosed up against the front window.

The narrow street was clogged with parked cars but a few

of the go-getters had already left for their offices and I was able to squeeze in close by. There was a trickle of traffic in the street, not much, and it was all quiet in the houses on either side of Glassop's.

I rang the bell but heard no sound. I knocked loudly, got no response and knocked again. I heard a shuffling and Glassop opened the door. He was in pyjamas and struggling to get one arm into a dressing-gown sleeve. Without his glasses, he peered at me myopically. His jaw dropped and he attempted to close the door but I pushed it fully open, shouldered him inside and closed the door.

'Not pleased to see me, Gordon? Why's that?'

'I ... I'm surprised, that's all.'

'I don't think it is all.'

I felt almost foolish doing it, but I took the .38 from my jacket pocket and tapped the barrel against his quivering chin.

'Jesus, what ...?'

You see pistols on TV and photos in newspapers, but if you've never seen and smelled one for real, up close, it can be a very scary thing. Glassop almost fainted. I put the gun away.

'Let's talk,' I said. 'You'd be ready for some coffee, right?'

I prodded him down the passage past a door on the left to the kitchen at the back of the house. It was untidy and smelled of take-out food, bad drainage and mould. He stood helplessly in the middle of the room, barefoot and with his dressing gown only half on.

'I . . . haven't got any proper coffee. Just instant.'

'That's all right. Just make some for yourself. Better put some sugar in it. You look peaky.'

'You scared me.'

'Be scared. Be very scared.'

That might have been overdoing it. He turned towards the sink, picked up a mug and reached for a tin of instant coffee near the stove. 'What do you want?'

'I want to know everything about your dealings with Sean Bright or Steve Ball or whatever he's calling himself.'

He dropped the mug and his fluttering hand knocked the tin of coffee to the floor.

'Now look what you've done,' I said.

'I didn't want . . . He threatened to . . .'

'I know, I know, but now you don't have to worry anymore.'

My evidence of Glassop's involvement with Bright was circumstantial at best but Glassop had confirmed it with his immediate admission. Bullying a weak person like him isn't edifying or enjoyable, but I had to keep it up until I had him completely under control. Fear is a great controller.

'Forget the coffee. Sit down.'

He stumbled to a chair at the kitchen table. I remained standing.

'You lied to the police about what happened at Wollongong.'

'I was terrified.'

'Doesn't matter. You're complicit in a kidnapping, if not a murder. And now you're cooperating with a blackmailer.'

'He told me what he'd do to me with this horrible knife he has.'

'Yeah, I know about the knife. You're not the only one he's threatened with it. He held it at Penelope's throat while he raped her.'

'That's what he threatened to do to me unless I agreed to help him. He told me I had to . . . do something when he gave the signal.'

'I understand. That's a nasty threat, but you can forget about him and get yourself clear of all this if you do what I say.'

I told him he had to produce all the material Bright had entrusted him with and talk to some people about what Bright had arranged with him.

'What people?'

'You'll see. You told me you kept everything of importance on a flash drive. Do you have this stuff in that form?'

He nodded.

'All the texts and phone calls?'

Another nod.

'Good. We're off to Canberra.'

'I'm not going to Canberra.'

'You are, Gordon, either willingly or unwillingly with your feet tied together and sitting on a plastic sheet.'

'A plastic sheet. Why?'

'It's a fair way. You might need to piss and you can't get to a toilet with your legs tied together, can you?'

Glassop cleaned himself up. He gave me the flash drive from his keyring and another he detached from one of the several computers he had in the second bedroom. I also took his mobile phone.

He protested. 'I need that. I've got clients.'

'What sort of clients?'

'None of your business.'

It was his first spark of resistance and I let him have it because I'd already snooped in the office while he was showering and seen that he was working as a mobile trouble-shooter for Mac computers.

I wasn't relishing spending a couple of hours with him but it couldn't be helped and I needed information. Once we were underway I asked him if he'd read the material Bright had assigned to him. He admitted that he had.

'Summarise it.'

'Come on, there's a ton of it.'

'Does it focus on one person in particular?'

'Three people really, but, yeah, one who's properly in the shit.'

'And that is?'

'This MP named Polkinghorn, who's a real scumbag.'

'What's he done?'

Glassop enjoyed detailing the misdeeds of others. 'You name it. He took bribes from pharmaceutical companies when he was Minister for Health and he connived with lawyers to inflate legal bills and took kickbacks.'

'Is there any one big thing in particular?'

'Do you call ten million bucks big?'

'Big enough.'

'That's what it cost an auditing firm for him to sign off on a shonky audit that kept a company afloat long enough for the directors to strip it and disappear.'

I switched off the voice recorder I had in my pocket. This sounded like the stuff Jones was after and he'd be glad to have the gist of it in Glassop's version.

'How long would it take for someone to work through the dirt?'

'All of it, or just Polkinghorn?'

'Just him.'

'Depends how good the person was.'

'Assuming he or she was good.'

'Could do it in a day. Does it matter?'

'With luck that's as long as you'll have to sit around after you turn the data over to a Mr Jones and brief him.'

He licked his lips, stared out the window at concrete and bush and said nothing.

'How much did Bright pay you?'

'Five grand.'

'How much did you charge O'Hara and Pen for the fake IDs?'

'Not much. Should've been more. Rory owes me money, but Penelope was paying.'

'I doubt you'll collect. O'Hara's broke.'

'Shit. How about you? This must be helping you. Must be worth something.'

I laughed. 'Mate, all you've done is save yourself from Bright and gaol. That's if everything works out right. Be grateful.'

'What do you mean, if it works out?'

It was my turn to shut up. I let him stew.

Twenty kilometres short of the ACT border I stopped at a service station to allow Glassop to have a piss. I checked the toilet and saw there was no way out but the way in.

'You think I'm going to try to run away?' he said.

'I don't know you well enough to tell what you'd do.'

'I've got no transport, no money. You're responsible for me.'

Strange thing for a grown man to say, but in a way Glassop wasn't fully grown and he certainly wasn't much of a man. While he was occupied, I called the number Jones had given me.

'Yes?'

'This is Hardy. I've got the man you want. He has all the data and he knows all about Polkinghorn—your target.'

If he was surprised that I knew that much he didn't show it. 'You've been busy. Where are you?'

'Not too far away.'

'Here's where I want you to bring him.'

'Forget it,' I said. 'I'm calling the shots now. I don't take him anywhere until you deposit Penelope back in our motel with her belongings and she phones me to say she's seen your guys drive away and that she's locked in and safe.'

'If I don't agree?'

'You will. I've got what you want. You can handle Bright and Polkinghorn any way you please. The backup man's defused now and he's bloody harmless. You might actually find some use for him. There isn't much he doesn't know about computers.'

There was a long pause before he spoke and I had a sense that he was conferring with other people. 'All right,' he said. 'These arrangements will take some time.'

'How long?'

'Miss Marinos will phone you at five o'clock.'

'Agreed.' More hours to kill in Glassop's company.

Jones liked to have the last word. 'Kyle Swan's not happy with you, Hardy. He has a suspected ruptured spleen.'

Poor Mr B, I thought. 'Kyle's got a soft mid-section,' I said. 'He needs to work out more and keep his tiny mind on the job.'

Glassop heard the last few exchanges. He fidgeted nervously. 'What now?'

'Sightseeing,' I said.

24

Killing time in Canberra on a cold winter's day isn't easy. We had a lunch neither of us wanted and drove up Black Mountain and around the lake. Glassop was sullen and apprehensive. I was preoccupied, trying to anticipate things ahead. We made a silent, unsociable pair.

I pulled into a car park and waited with the engine running for the heater. My phone rang at five precisely.

'Hardy.'

'It's me,' Pen said. 'I'm in the motel. I saw the creep who delivered me drive off.'

'Have you got the door locked?'

'Locked and on the chain.'

'What name are you going by?'

'My name.'

'Marinos?'

'Yes. What are you doing?'

'What's Jones told you?'

'I haven't seen Jones since you left me in their care. I haven't been told anything.'

'I'll tell you when I see you.'

'Thanks a lot.'

She hung up. I swore and shook my head.

'What's wrong?' Glassop said.

'Nothing that concerns you.'

The phone rang again. Jones. I confirmed that I'd heard from Pen. He instructed me to drive to Fyshwick, Canberra's industrial precinct, where I'd be met. I took the road to the airport as darkness fell.

'Jesus, don't tell me we're flying somewhere. I'm scared of flying.'

'Don't worry.'

I passed the airport and when I made the turn into Fyshwick a parked Volvo flashed its lights. It pulled out and I followed it through the quiet streets as the factories and workshops closed for the day. The Volvo stopped at a guarded gate in a high cyclone fence. The fence enclosed a compound with a large building like a warehouse in the centre and several vehicles neatly parked. The compound was lit by powerful lamps mounted on high poles in each corner. The guard waved the Volvo through and I followed.

Glassop was licking his lips furiously. 'Where are we? What's this place?'

'I don't know,' I said. I put my hand in the deep pocket of my leather jacket.

'You've got that bloody gun, haven't you? I think I'm going to be sick.'

I parked beside the Volvo. The driver got out and beckoned us to follow him. The air was freezing and I could hear Glassop's teeth chattering as I hauled him across the bitumen to a door in the building. The driver opened it and shepherded us inside.

Plain outside, the inside of the building showed signs of money having been spent. There was a large reception area with high-tech desk, pigeonholes and a few tasteful prints on the walls. Polished tiles on the floor, a coffee table, comfortable-looking chairs, a rack of newspapers, a pile of magazines, muted lighting, almost silent air-conditioning.

Jones, in his immaculate suit and minus the gun bulge, came towards us.

I reached into my pocket for the flash drives and held them out for Jones. 'This is Gordon Glassop,' I said. 'This bloke goes by the name of Jones, Gordon. God knows what his real name is.'

'Please take the drives, Mr Glassop, and come with me.'

I gave the drives to Glassop. His hand was damp.

'Have you got Bright?' I said.

Jones nodded.

'Give you any trouble?'

'A little. Wait here. I'll ask Mr Glassop a few questions and then put him to work. I'll see you when I'm ready.'

I took the voice recorder out, pressed the buttons and played the first few words of Glassop's statement. Glassop stared at me with a look that would have been angry if he hadn't been so frightened.

'The gist,' I said.

I tossed the recorder to Jones, who caught it neatly. He gestured to the waiting area and steered Glassop towards a wide spiral staircase.

I took a seat and picked up a magazine—*Business Today*. I put it down and riffled through the pile but they were all business magazines. There were cameras mounted high on the walls and I'd have been willing to bet there were bugs in the furniture. I strolled over to the desk, which held a computer, two telephones and an electronic device I couldn't identify. I picked it up and a robotic voice said, *Please do not touch.*

I browsed the newspapers and tapped my feet. If I'd been a nail-chewer I'd have chewed my nails, if I'd been a lip-licker I'd have licked my lips. But all I could do was hum half-forgotten songs and nurse my impatience. I thought of calling Pen but didn't. There'd been nothing remotely welcoming in her tone.

After more than an hour Jones came down the stairs. He sat in a chair opposite me and held out his hand. I didn't shake it.

'No need to be like that, Hardy. You did a great job, quick, too.'

'That's me. How do things stack up?'

'Very well indeed. Your Mr Glassop is very talented. He teased out all sorts of things that whoever encrypted the material, I assume Ms Marinos, appears to have tried to hide. Things Bright also got on to, very damaging things that he was prepared to use.'

'Bully for Gordon. Now what?'

'To use your expression, Glassop is defused and so is Bright. We convinced him he has no cards to play now. I'm offering Mr Glassop a position in our organisation. I think he'll accept.'

'What about Polkinghorn?'

'All our suspicions were confirmed. The dishonourable Tim Polkinghorn's career is severely compromised, shall we say. And our clients may well adopt a different stance towards him and others. All in all, a very satisfactory result.'

'So glad. You said Bright gave you trouble.'

'With his martial arts talents, yes. He did a certain amount of damage to one of our people but he was restrained.'

'Is he hurt?'

'Oh, no.'

I patted my jacket pocket for reassurance.

'You're armed, I see. You were scanned as you came in.'

'Right. So now we call the police.'

He shook his head.

'No, I guess not,' I said. 'You don't want cops poking around here. Okay, hand him over to me.'

'I'm afraid not. He was of no further use to us and no threat.'

'What're you saying?'

'We let him go.'

'For Christ's sake, why?'

'He may be useful in the future.'

part three

25

I threatened Jones with a charge of enforced restraint and he replied by saying he was sure he could persuade Glassop to level a similar charge against me. Stalemate there. All Jones would say was that Bright had left by taxi.

'How much money did he have?'

'No idea.'

'I can't help wondering whether you employed him in the first place and he went rogue.'

'Wonder away.'

'That's a lot of dirt you've got now.'

'I'm sure we'll find a use for it.'

'I won't wish you luck.'

'Luck, Mr Hardy, is for those without brains.'

'How's Kyle?'

'He'll mend, but you've made an enemy there.'

'He can stand in line.'

'I have to say Bright made several threats as well.'

'He wouldn't know where Penelope is, would he?'

Jones shrugged. 'Who can say? There's been a lot of coming and going. He may have overheard something.'

'If she's come to any harm I'll be back.'

'Come back by all means, but I doubt you'll find a Mr Jones here.'

I went out. My breath plumed in the freezing air. I drove to the motel and asked at reception for Ms Marinos's room. The receptionist was not the one I'd dealt with before.

'I'm sorry, sir,' the woman said. 'Ms Marinos has checked out.'

'When?'

'I can't tell you that. It's—'

I showed her my PIA licence and put on my most serious manner. She tapped computer keys.

'At five-thirty-five.'

'Was she alone?'

I must have sounded threatening because she merely nodded.

'You called her a taxi, right?'

'Yes.'

'Where was she going?'

'To the airport. Is . . . is something wrong?'

I didn't answer. I left and sat in the car feeling a wave of disappointment and apprehension rushing towards me. Bright and Pen both gone and I had no idea where. *Great work, Hardy,* I thought. *Neville Kim'll be thrilled to hear all about it.*

I had dinner where Glassop and I had eaten lunch simply because I couldn't be bothered looking for anything else. The food—swordfish, salad and chips—was surprisingly good and that, with a glass of wine, made me feel more cheerful. I told myself again that finding people was my go and I was convinced of it after the second glass.

I had coffee and, rugged up with a scarf and gloves, I walked around for a while until I was sure I was safe to drive. I'd had enough of Canberra and the ACT. I drove to Queanbeyan over the border into New South Wales and checked into a motel. I drank the rest of the bottle of wine, watched television and went to bed. I'd only slept with Pen for a couple of nights, but it was enough to make me miss her.

I ate breakfast in the motel dining room, stoked up on black coffee and felt alert as I took the road to Gundaroo. I was pretty sure Bright wouldn't be there, but my idea was to look over his cottage to see if he'd left any clue as to where he might have gone.

Nothing much was stirring in the frosty morning in Gundaroo. I drove out to Bright's place where again there was no sign of a car. This time I pushed open the rickety gate and drove right up to the house. There was no traffic on the road and the nearest house was a good distance away. I thought I'd be undisturbed for long enough.

The cottage was in poor repair with a sagging bullnose veranda, at least one window boarded up, and rusty guttering. Two decayed car bodies stood in long grass beside the place; the wooden porch slumped where its brick underpinnings had given way. The flyscreen was a tattered ruin. The front door opened creakingly on protesting hinges.

I walked through quickly to get the layout—central passage, two bedrooms, kitchen-cum-living room with a big fireplace. The back door opened on a fenced yard. A fibro and corrugated iron lean-to held a washhouse with a copper and a sink. There was a vegetable patch and a chook pen in the yard, now both overgrown. Some heavy plastic sheeting had been tacked up to provide a covered sitting area where there was a cane chair, a milk crate full of empty beer stubbies and a plastic garden pot where a plant of some kind was trying to draw nourishment from hundreds of cigarette butts.

One bedroom was full of junked furniture; the other held a double bed covered with a stained blanket. No sheets, no pillow. I'd seen dossing places like this before—typically, the occupant used a sleeping bag and rolled up clothes for a pillow. A length of electrical cable ran from a nail in the doorjamb to the shaft of a floor lamp that lacked a bulb and shade. A couple of empty wire coat hangers dangled from the cable.

The barman had told me Bright drove a Jeep, a not inexpensive car. Why would he live in a place like this and over time as the barman had said, even intermittently? The question stayed with me as I searched the kitchen-cum-living room where he'd obviously spent most of his time. There were ashes in the fireplace and the remnants of a stack of chopped wood. There was an old refrigerator, a combustion stove and some shelves still holding tins of soup and cans of tuna and sardines.

All the signs were of a hasty departure—milk and cheese and bowls of leftover food in the fridge, cutlery and plates in the sink and a half-full stubby of VB on the table. A moth-eaten armchair was drawn up near the combustion stove and, wedged down between the cushions, I found a crumpled magazine. *Love in Chains* was a BDSM publication with a snuff element incorporated. The stories and photographs involved young women variously restrained and penetrated by leather-clad, masked men—personally, or using implements. A number of the photo sequences, presumably faked, ended with the females dead and the men masturbating over their inert bodies.

I went out into the yard for some fresh air and became aware of a smell. I walked towards the chook pen at the end of the yard and disturbed a dog that had been scratching in the dirt inside the derelict structure. It came towards me growling and baring its teeth. I picked up a heavy stick and swiped at it intending to just miss. But it jumped forward and I hit it hard on the nose. It yelped and ran away, scrambling under the fence where it seemed to have recently dug a hole.

Still holding the stick, I crouched to duck under a remaining roof strut to investigate where the dog had been scratching. It had dug deep under layers of chook shit and soil and cleared a sizeable area, exposing two human skulls and several bones. One of the skulls still had flesh adhering to it—the source of the smell. I turned away and forced myself not to vomit. The skulls weren't man-sized or child-sized. They were the remains of women.

26

The police found the skeletons of five young women buried in the yard of the Gundaroo house. Under the floorboards they found clothes, shoes and accessories. The remains showed signs of torture and dismemberment. Charred human bones were found in the combustion stove, and a fatty residue in a copper in the washhouse was evidence of human flesh having been boiled.

I told the police who I was working for and how I'd traced Bright or Ball to Gundaroo. I didn't say anything about Pen or Jones or Glassop. They asked why, since I'd got the information from the barman the day before, I'd let so much time elapse before searching the house. I said that the house appeared empty the first time I'd looked at it and I waited a day to confirm this—true as far as it went.

They were unhappy with me carrying out an investigation without informing them of my presence and for not notifying them of a wanted criminal in the area—and for being an armed trespasser—but as I'd turned up evidence of a major crime they weren't in a position to protest. I was held in uncomfortable rooms, interrogated in a hostile manner and had my car and my belongings searched. But when Neville Kim confirmed my story in every detail they had no course but to release me, although I was obliged to stay in Queanbeyan for several days while they checked everything.

'So you have no idea where this bastard's gone?' one of the detectives asked in the last interview.

'That's right.'

'You wouldn't be holding out like you did before, hoping to get the glory for yourself?'

'Glory's not an asset in my business.'

In fact, the story made headlines in the eastern states and ran for longer than usual as the women were identified. Two were Canberra prostitutes in the low-income bracket; one was a British backpacker and the other two were from the tribe of itinerant workers that travel the country districts— fruit-pickers, vineyard and market-garden casuals—who easily slip through the cracks. I dropped out of the story early, but still got more exposure, not all of it complimentary, than I wanted. I shifted motels twice to avoid reporters. It didn't work.

Early on, Neville Kim rang to thank me.

'What for?' I said. 'I came close but he got away.'

'The police are redoubling their efforts or, I should say, are now making an effort. The photograph of the man is much clearer now that some technology has been applied to it, and it's being widely circulated. I am optimistic but I want you to continue.'

'Mr Kim, it's already cost you a lot of money and I don't have any leads. I—'

'As I say, you have achieved something. The discovery of the bodies of those unfortunate women must have been a shock. When you've recovered from that you may think of something.'

'You're paying me to *think*?'

'I do it all the time. Draw on the funds I've provided. God bless you.'

So he was one of the Christian Koreans. Perhaps he was praying as well as paying for me. Before leaving Queanbeyan I rang Glassop's mobile and the number Jones had given me. No answer in both cases. I was packed and ready to go when the phone in the motel room rang. I answered; the caller was a woman with an English accent.

'Mr Hardy, I'm the mother of Gloria Drake, one of the murdered girls.'

'Mrs Drake, I'm sorry.'

'Yes, but I wanted to thank you. We've been driven almost insane by not knowing what happened to Gloria. My husband and I travelled from England and we've been here for two years making inquiries. Now we know. It's terrible but it's better in a way.'

'I understand.'

'I wish we had come to you in the first place. Thank you again.'

I put the phone down although I felt like throwing it through the window. I realised that I'd hardly given any thought to the murdered girls and their families. I'd been too busy being economical with the truth to the police and fending off reporters. And me with a daughter of my own. I was feeling their pain now and an urgent need to see Megan and Ben. And something else—I wanted to get Sean Bright more than I'd wanted anything for a long time.

I stopped in Newtown but Megan wasn't at home. I could have phoned or texted but I wanted to see and touch both her and Ben—an unusually needy feeling for me. I drove to Glebe in this mood and my pulse went up a few notches when I saw Pen's car parked in the street.

She greeted me with a hug that bent my ribs. I returned it and clung to her speechlessly.

'I'm sorry I was such a shit in Canberra,' she said when we finally broke apart. 'I felt abandoned and I was scared.'

'It was bad,' I said. 'All bad, but they didn't hurt you, did they?'

She shook her head. 'No, but I felt like a pawn in a game that just you and they were playing and . . .'

'It's all right,' I said.

SILENT KILL

She pointed to a pile of newspapers on the coffee table. 'I got here feeling buggered and angry and thought I'd just sleep one night and take off. I got the horrors when the news broke and I bloody nearly collapsed. I was under that man's control for days.'

'I thought about that, too.'

'Then I started to think what you'd gone through and I felt rotten. So I stayed.'

We went upstairs to bed and remained there for the rest of the day.

In the evening, I told Pen about Glassop and my dealings with Jones at Fyshwick—all the stuff that wasn't in the newspapers. She listened and nodded in the appropriate places but she seemed distracted.

'Are you okay, Pen?' I asked.

'I don't know.'

'Tell me.'

We were in the kitchen eating a cheese omelette, one of my few culinary achievements, and drinking red wine. She had her appetite back and was going easy on the wine. She took a swig and put her glass down.

'I'm fine, sort of,' she said. 'I'm over the rape and all the rest of it.'

'What, then?'

217

'It's you. I'm not asking you to tell me how you feel about me. I know men hate that kind of question. It's how I feel about you and it's not good. I feel as if I might fall apart again without you, and I hate that feeling. It makes me want to . . .'

'Do what?'

'Go . . .'

'Where?'

'I don't know and I don't know if I could. That's the bugger of it. I can't just . . . I have to do *something*. I feel as if I've left all sorts of things hanging in mid-air, and I don't even know what they are.'

You haven't got over anything, I thought, but I didn't say it and I didn't know how to help her.

She scraped the scraps on her plate into the bin and rinsed the plate. 'When my swimming career went bung I saw a psychologist. She was helpful. If she's still around I think I'll see her again.'

'Sounds like a good idea.'

'Sounds like a good idea,' she mocked. 'Oh, shit, Cliff, I'm sorry. I didn't mean to . . .'

'It's all right.'

'No, it's not all right. What are you going to do?'

'I'm going to find Bright.'

She refilled her glass and toasted me. 'A man with a purpose.'

27

The next day Pen located her psychologist and went off to see her in Bondi Junction. After a quick visit to Megan and Ben, I went to my office and dealt with routine things. My media exposure hadn't led to a flood of clients. Megan said that Ben had seen me on television when a crew caught up with me in Queanbeyan.

'What's Cliff doing?' Ben had asked.

'Hiding,' Megan said.

'Why?'

Ben was at that stage when kids ask why exhaustively, whatever the answer they receive, and after three more whys Megan had persuaded him to stop and play with his toys.

I sat at my desk with a notebook in which I'd jotted down various things during the course of the investigation, plus the printouts Pen had prepared, and made more notes of things half-remembered that Jack Buchanan, Rory O'Hara, Kelly,

Pen, Glassop and Jones had said. I pored over the material, hoping to see something that would point me in the direction of Bright. Some unanswered or unasked question. The only thing I came up with was the matter of who had hired Bright in the first place, or had he been freelance from the start?

Not helpful. I stared at the wall, so frustrated and pre-occupied that I barely heard my mobile ring. It was in the pocket of my jacket, which I'd hung on the back of the door. I swore and heaved myself up, prepared to be unpleasant.

'Hardy.'

'This is Jones. I think we should meet.'

'Why?'

'I imagine you want to find Bright.'

'I do.'

'I may be able to help you.'

'Why would you?'

'I'll explain. I'm at the Novotel in Darling Harbour. Shall we say in the coffee shop in an hour?'

It wasn't far, the day was mild, so I walked. The Novotel is no uglier than other buildings of its kind, and it offered all the homogenised comforts international travellers demand. The coffee shop was on the mezzanine floor and I found Jones sitting at a table reading a newspaper. The man who'd introduced himself as Mr A was sitting with him and alerted him to my arrival. Jones nodded and put the paper down.

'Barney,' Jones said, 'why don't you go and see the sights for a while?'

'Barney who?' I said.

'Just Barney.'

I sat down. 'Like you're just Jones.'

'Yes.'

Barney gave me an unfriendly look and moved off. Jones reached into his jacket pocket and brought out my voice recorder. He slid it across the table.

'Very helpful, thank you, but I don't suggest you record this conversation. Coffee?'

'Flat white,' I said. 'Very hot.'

'I agree.' Jones signalled for a waiter and ordered the coffee.

'You made a splash in the media,' Jones said.

'It couldn't be helped.'

'I was grateful that you didn't refer to our . . . business.'

'Don't be grateful. I was protecting myself from a charge of withholding information about a wanted man. It could've meant my licence. As I told you, I have enemies.'

The coffee came and we stirred and drank.

'Let's get to it,' I said. 'Why have you come out of the shadows, as it were?'

'I wouldn't put it quite like that, but do you remember asking me whether my organisation had employed Bright?'

'Yeah, you ducked the question.'

'That was before you revealed what sort of monster he

is. Well, we didn't use him on that particular job, but we did recommend him to an . . . affiliate organisation.'

'So you feel some responsibility for the death of Melanie Kim?'

Jones shook his head. 'No, certainly not directly. That's something we would not have tolerated.'

'Of course not. You just assault and kidnap people.'

'Have your fun, Hardy. No, but I do feel some responsibility on account of those women he killed and what he might do in the future.'

'You should.'

'Perhaps. Anyway, as things stand, he went rogue, to use your phrase, probably triggered by the Kim killing. I want to help you if I can.'

'So far all you've done is talk and buy me coffee. Start helping.'

'You're a difficult man to deal with, Hardy.'

'Listen, I don't like you. I don't like corporations and corporate fixers and lobbyists and lawyers and the whole shonky crew you're a part of.'

'You're a primitive. Don't you realise how corporatised the world has become? Everything is outsourced and contracted to big organisations.'

'Yeah, to avoid responsibility and accountability.'

'You and your kind are dinosaurs, on the way to extinction.'

'Maybe, but we'll get up the noses of people like you and have some fun while we're still around. I'll finish my coffee and be on my way unless you've got something useful to say.'

'We did use him on several other jobs—industrial espionage, I suppose you'd call it. His real name is Stefan Balakin. He's a former Australian intelligence officer. I imagine that if you have contacts in the intelligence community they would be able to give you more information.'

'The intelligence community doesn't give out information.'

'You've proved your resourcefulness. I suggest you prove it some more. That's all I have to tell you.'

He got up and, as if by magic, Barney appeared in the coffee shop. Jones gestured to him to pay for the coffee, which he did. Then the two of them left. I remained in my seat, swilling the dregs of the flat white in my cup.

I'd tried to avoid dealing with intelligence people, but inevitably I'd run up against a few over the years. Most of them I disliked and distrusted. They performed non-jobs, wasted enormous amounts of public money and were only accountable to people playing the same meaningless game higher up the pole. There were exceptions—occasional genuinely useful operations that headed off disasters. There was also the odd agent who bucked the system and lived in the real world and focused on protecting innocent people and making life difficult for guilty ones.

Josh Carey was like that. He'd resisted promotion into the managerial ranks and concentrated his energies on putting fanatics out of business and resolving disputes between different factions in ethnic communities before they got out of hand. He was a maverick within the service, tough and intelligent, and he spoke about ten languages. He'd helped me some years back in a case that could have spiralled into an 'honour killing' nightmare without his intervention.

There was something compatible between us and we met for a drink from time to time, but not in the last year. With Carey, there was always the chance that he'd been eased out, but it was worth a try. After walking back to my office and finding, as I'd expected, that Jones had wiped the voice recording, I rang Carey's mobile.

'Carey.'

'Are you sure? Better check your file on yourself.'

'Cliff Hardy. I had a feeling I might be hearing from you.'

That was Carey, smart as they came. I could imagine his superiors' irritation at his lightning-fast ability to absorb facts and make intuitive leaps. He knew straight off what I wanted to talk about so there was no need to mention names, which we wouldn't have done over the phone anyway. He was in Sydney as part of a team discussing intelligence agency transparency with a similar group from another country, which he didn't name. He said he could squeeze out a free hour or so. He was staying at a hotel in the Rocks and proposed meeting me at Circular Quay mid-afternoon.

'Why there?'

'So we can catch a ferry to Manly.'

'Why Manly?'

'I want the guy who'll be tailing me to see the sights. They tell me sometimes there's penguins on Manly Beach. I doubt he'd ever have seen a penguin.'

'Right,' I said. 'There was a whale with a calf in the harbour the other day. Might still be there.'

'Even better, though I suspect he'd rather eat it than watch it.'

'Okay, the Quay it is. *Sayonara.*'

'Close,' Carey said.

The day had turned cool and blustery and there was rain in the air. The ferries pulling into the Quay bucked and heaved with the swell until firmly moored. I waited just outside the terminal, early as usual. I saw Carey approaching from the far end of the concourse and calculated that he'd arrive at three-fifty, exactly the time he'd suggested. He was a great one for precise times and punctuality. I'd tackled him once on this, saying it made him predictable.

'I can be as late as Oscar Wilde or as early as you when it matters,' he'd said.

I was looking at my watch as he strode up. Carey was tall and lean with thinning hair and a waistline kept trim by squash. He'd invited me to play with him once but I'd declined; I knew he'd be tigerish in a tight space. I'd countered with an offer to play tennis but he said the game was too slow. Now we shook hands and went to buy our tickets. The Manly ferry left in three minutes.

'You checked,' I said.

'Of course, didn't you?'

'I've got more time to spare. Have you spotted your tail?'

'She's there. She's pretty good.'

'But you're better?'

'Older.'

The ferry pulled in, splashing the unwary who stood too close to the edge of the wharf. Carey was wearing an overcoat and scarf and I had on my heavy leather jacket with the collar turned up, so we were able to stand out on a fairly protected section of the deck, but still a bit huddled with our hands in our pockets.

It was going to be a rough ride; the swell was high and the engines churned hard, battling it. We weren't alone on the outside—claustrophobics, those sensitive to the diesel fumes and shutterbugs hoping for whales, or at least dolphins, were clinging to the rails.

'Stefan Balakin,' Carey said.

'You recognised him from the photo in the paper.'

'Only just. He's something of a chameleon. He was bulkier when he was with . . . us, and had much longer hair.'

'Your mob must have a complete file on him—background, habits, secrets . . .'

'Closed, very closed. So closed the media never got a sniff because the people who regularly leak to the media didn't have a clue. In any case Balakin was always sort of peripheral, almost a freelance, like a newspaper stringer in a way.'

'The file isn't closed to you is it, Josh?'

'No. I took a look, but it's surprisingly sparse. Balakin's parents were Russians, of course, got out in the seventies when things were loosening up. Balakin was born here and recruited after university in 1993 when he was twenty-one. Bilingual from the cradle, very useful.'

'Did you work with him?'

'Once, when there was a Ukrainian scare in Melbourne, a factional thing that threatened to blow up big.'

'Was he any good?'

'Yes and no. Violent. A woman died.'

'I need to know everything about him—what he's likely to do, where he's likely to go.'

Carey nodded. 'I'll tell you what I can, but you have to know what you're up against.'

'I've met him. I know what he's done. I know he's a martial arts expert and can be charming when he wants to be.'

The ferry ploughed through the waves towards Manly. Exposed in mid-harbour, with the wind whistling and blowing spray from the crests of the waves, the deck travellers retreated inside and Carey and I did the same so as not to be conspicuous as the only on-deckers.

I glanced at the other passengers. There were lots of Asian faces, as there are everywhere in Sydney, and the full range of humanity—families, adolescents, men and women singly and in groups. I spotted at least three candidates for Carey's tail. There was no way to know who was the right one, but I was sure Carey knew. He seemed oddly reluctant to add to what he'd said. His narrow, lined face was set hard and he pulled a bunch of tissues from his pocket and dabbed at his nose.

'Bloody cold coming on,' he said.

'Come on, Josh, you were saying . . .'

He sniffed. 'I'm not the only spook who spotted Balakin.'

'Okay, so?'

'They move slowly but they do move. Cliff, there's no way the powers that be can allow it to get out that a former intelligence agent is a sadistic serial murderer.'

'You mean they'll be looking for him as well? That had crossed my mind.'

'More than that. The aim will be to remove him in total secrecy, erase him in what's called a silent kill.'

28

Carey said that in rare instances the intelligence chiefs sanctioned the removal, leaving no body, witnesses or clues, of people whose existence constituted a serious threat.

'To national security?' I said, although I knew otherwise.

He nodded. 'Yes, but more often to the organisation itself.'

'I've wondered about a few cases,' I said.

'Sometimes it's botched and then there has to be a cover-up, usually poorly managed. I'm sure Balakin will be targeted this way. I doubt anyone has been assigned to the job, but there will certainly have been a beefing-up of the controls—airport checks, shipping departures, credit-card usage, that sort of thing.'

'So I could just sit back and let it happen?'

'You could, but you'd never know.'

'I've got a client who wants closure.'

'Is that all?'

'No, it's personal, too.'

'I thought so.'

'Meaning?'

'You've got a certain look. Last time it was all about a woman. How about now?'

We'd reached the Manly wharf, and joined the passengers shuffling off. It was my turn to delay a response. How much did I want to get Bright for what he'd done to Pen and how much was it a professional exercise? Not for the first time, I didn't know.

We hadn't seen any whales or dolphins and there weren't any penguins on the beach. We strolled along the Corso, each with a packet of chips.

'Well?' Carey said.

'What does it matter? Yeah, there's a woman involved. I've got a question for you. If I was to get to Balakin first and everything about him was exposed, how would you feel about that, you being the dissident you are?'

We stopped and Carey flicked a couple of chips at a flutter of seagulls. 'Get real, Cliff. If you got there first, steps would be taken to make sure you hadn't got there at all.'

'I'd be careful.'

'You'd better be.' He paused. 'I knew I wouldn't be able to put you off. I've been trying to think of something about him that mightn't be on the file, or not obviously, to give you an advantage.'

'I'd be grateful, Josh.'

'The only thing I've been able to come up with is chess.'

'He plays chess? That'd be on his file, surely?'

'Yes, but listen. I happened to mention that I played a bit and he challenged me to a game. He beat me and won a fair bit of my money.'

'You played for money?'

'He insisted on it. Said he only ever played for money.'

'Isn't that unusual?'

'It is, but the really funny thing was he insisted on speaking Russian throughout the game. I speak pretty good Russian so it wasn't a problem, but he said he could only play chess when thinking and speaking in Russian. From the way he played I'd say he was an addict. They get that way, like bridge players.'

'Really addicted?'

'Yeah, there's something about chess and bridge that's compulsive, apparently, especially for good players. I don't know if there's a name for it, but it applies to crossword doers as well. You ever know anyone who did cryptic crosswords?'

'I do, my sister. She was super bright, smarter than me. She began doing them when she was still in primary school. She couldn't start the day until she'd at least made some progress with the cryptic. Made her late for school sometimes. Drove our mother nuts.'

'That's it. I bet she still does them.'

I saw my sister and my nephew and niece infrequently. They lived in New Zealand and I didn't go there often. I'd last paid them a visit a couple of years ago and, sure enough, she was doing the cryptic while getting breakfast for her kids.

'You're right, she does. So I have to look for somewhere Russian-speakers play chess?'

'At a very high level. Do you play chess, Cliff?'

'No, and I don't play bridge or do cryptic crosswords. I'm a linear thinker.'

'You're lazy,' Carey said. 'Push yourself, you'll need to.'

Both waistline-conscious, we fed most of the chips to the seagulls before catching a ferry back to the Quay. I amused myself by trying to spot Carey's tail and played it like a guessing game: *Blue scarf? Brown jacket? Beret?* I was wrong every time, or so he said.

I walked back to where I'd parked my car near the office and drove to Glebe. I knew there was trouble brewing when I hung up my scarf and jacket on the hallstand and saw the spare key sitting there. I'd brought the boots in from the car hoping to strike an interesting note, but it was a wrong move.

Pen was sitting in the living room with her knees drawn up and a tight smile on her face that disappeared when she saw the boots.

'What?' I said.

'You want me to put them on? Want to take a photo?'

I was tired, cold and frustrated and I wanted a drink. I threw the boots onto the couch. 'No, yes, if you want to.'

Her laugh ended in a despairing sob. 'Do you know how . . . used . . . I felt when you had me dress up like that?'

'You didn't seem to mind at the time.'

'That's part of it.'

'Not as used as when . . .'

'Worse, in a way.'

I moved towards her but she stood and put up her hands with fists clenched.

'Pen, what's happened?'

'Lavinia says I have to get away from you and this whole mess.'

'Lavinia's the psychologist?'

'Yes.' Pen picked up the bag she'd left at the bottom of the stairs and moved towards the passage. 'I'm sorry, Cliff.'

I nodded. 'Where will you go?'

'I'll be all right.'

'I'll get him,' I said.

She turned back and for a second I thought she was going to change her mind but she just had a last look around the room.

'I know you will,' she said. 'And you'll kill him or try to or someone else will and you'll think you've done a good job.'

'I don't understand.'

'I know, and you never will.'

I could hear her sobbing as she went down the passage. She closed the door quietly behind her and I stood there listening to the sound of the engine starting and her car moving slowly away.

29

I didn't break things and I didn't get drunk. I put the boots in a cupboard and went on a long walk through Jubilee Park and up through Annandale. The early part of the walk took me along Blackwattle Bay past the giant Moreton Bay figs. Something about the old, massive solidity of those trees comforted me. They'd survived major changes—the homeless camped in the shelter they provided during the Depression, the rejuvenation of the park and now the yuppies drinking champagne under their branches at birthday parties.

The walk tired me so much I stopped thinking about Pen and Balakin and everything else. I ate a sandwich, drank one glass of wine with my pills and fell into bed and a deep, dreamless sleep. If Pen had left a scent I didn't notice. She hadn't left her black slip.

In the morning when I booted up the computer there was a message from her: *Don't look for me.*

I spent some time on the web searching for chess clubs in Sydney, particularly near Bondi where Pen had said Bright had known his way around like the back of his hand. I rang a few, got voicemail from two and at the one that answered the man exhibited shock when I mentioned playing for money.

'None of our members plays for money,' he said.

'Doesn't anyone play chess for money? I thought Bobby Fischer made a fortune.'

'Of course it happens in big international tournaments, but you were asking about the local scene, weren't you?'

'Yes.'

His tone was sniffy. 'It happens in cafés around the place. Ethnic cafés, if you know what I mean.'

I did and I started Googling in my amateurish way, usually needing to revise a question three or four times to get a result. After a bit of this scrambling I came up with something promising—the Kiev Café in Bondi Road advertised itself as the home of Russian cuisine combined with facilities for 'competitive social chess'.

I filled in the day with a gym visit, and reading about chess and Russian customs. I tried to think of strategies I'd use if I actually found Balakin in the café or, more likely, if I learned things that helped me to find him. In particular, I had two things to worry about—his hapkido and his knife.

At 8 pm I parked in a side street off Bondi Road and

walked back to the café, which was upstairs through a narrow entrance slotted between a patisserie and a bottle shop, both doing good evening business. It looked the kind of place, like the Marinos restaurant, where the proprietor lives above where the money is made. I went up the stairs and into a fairly large room with about ten tables, a bar and what my reading had told me was a samovar. There were posters of Russian scenes on the walls and notices in Cyrillic script. Couples and groups of three or four were eating at half the tables and at three others men were bent over chessboards. A rack along one wall held several chessboards and boxes of chessmen. No Stefan Balakin.

I sat at one of the empty tables and ordered a glass of red wine. One waiter was doing all the work. He was fat and bald with a fierce moustache and a brusque manner.

'The kitchen is closing in ten minutes,' he said. 'Do you wish to eat?'

'No, thanks.'

'Are you intending to play? You are waiting for someone, perhaps?'

'Perhaps.'

He shrugged, went to the bar and poured the wine. He brought it to me, hovered for a few seconds and walked away. Several of the diners looked at me curiously; the chess players didn't. I drank some of the wine, which wasn't very good. I got the newspaper photograph of Bright/Balakin from my wallet and put it on the table along with my PIA licence.

The waiter couldn't resist. He came over with a cloth to wipe nonexistent spots from the empty table next to me.

There was a buzz of conversation from the diners loud enough to keep what I said to the waiter private. I took out a $50 note and caught his eye.

'I'm looking for this man.' I put my finger on the photo. 'Do you know him?'

He glanced around the room but said nothing. I added another fifty. He was tempted but he resisted.

'Police?'

'No,' I said.

'Probably something more bad. Go away.'

'There could be more money.'

'Drink your wine and leave!' He flicked the towel, sending the photo, money and licence folder to the floor. I collected the things, preserving as much dignity as you can bent double. One of the chess players picked up the photo, which had drifted towards his table. He looked at it briefly before returning it. I thanked him, left the wine and walked out.

The waiter's reaction seemed excessive to me. I thought about it as I made my way back to the car. If the waiter did know Balakin, talked to him and described me to him, Balakin would know who I was. That could be a good thing if I was willing to be the Judas goat. Was I? I wasn't sure.

When I reached the dark street where I'd parked I became aware of someone close behind me. Had the waiter had time to contact Balakin and put him on my track? Only if

Balakin had been close by. Or had Balakin simply been in the vicinity and spotted me? I tensed myself for an attack. I didn't reach for my keys. A street fighter keeps his arms loose and his hands free. When I sensed the person was less than a couple of metres away I spun around and stepped forward. Momentum is everything.

It wasn't Balakin. The young man halted and held a hand up defensively, making a cringing half turn away from my aggressive advance.

'Jesus,' he gasped, 'go easy.'

I stepped back and let him straighten up. There wasn't much light in the street, but up close I saw enough to recognise him as the one who'd picked up the photo of Balakin from the floor.

'You scared the shit out of me,' he said.

'Dark street, late night. Dumb behaviour on your part. You know Stefan Balakin, don't you?'

'What if I do?'

I took out my licence and let my jacket fall open so he could see the holstered pistol.

'I need to find him,' I said. 'And if you help me I won't have you charged with assault or do unpleasant things to you right here and now.'

'How about the money? I saw you flashing a hundred bucks.'

'That's more like it,' I said. 'Let's talk.'

We went to a coffee shop in Bondi Road. He told me his

name was Vane Goldman, that his mother was Russian and that he played regularly at the Kiev Café for money.

'I played this guy, the one in your photograph, a couple of weeks ago and beat him. He lost five hundred bucks.'

'You must be good.'

'I am.'

'And he only spoke Russian while you were playing?'

'That's right. How did you know?'

'I know. Why did you come after me?'

'I'm sorry. I was frustrated. I just wanted to talk to you, see what you were on about. Stefan said he'd pay me and he hasn't. I need the money. I'm a student and winning money at chess is how I keep going, partly.'

'Have you got any way of getting in touch with him?'

He'd regained his confidence but not all of it. He looked down into his cup. 'What's in it for me?'

'What're you studying?'

'I'm doing law at New South.'

'Perfect fit.' I took $200 from my wallet and passed it to him.

He grabbed the money. 'If you shoot him I'm out three hundred bucks.'

'I'm not going to shoot him. I'll pay you the rest when I hear something useful.'

'He ... he's thinner than in that photo. He looks a bit different.'

'I know that. Does he have a regular night at the café?'

Goldman thought about it. 'I played him on a Thursday. That's one of my regular nights. I think I saw him there the Thursday before. Yeah, I did. He was winning that night but I thought I'd be able to beat him. His opening—'

'Don't bother, I wouldn't understand.'

'One other thing I can tell you is that he has this knife strapped to his forearm.'

'Which forearm?'

He considered. 'The right, I think. He's a scary guy.'

'You weren't scared to tackle me.'

He shrugged. 'You're older. I didn't know you had a gun and I didn't realise you'd be so quick and hard.'

I paid for the coffees and took him along to an ATM, where I drew out more of Neville Kim's money. I gave Goldman another $300 and told him to stay away from the café.

'What's it all about?' he said.

'You don't need to know, Alfie.'

'Alfie?'

'A joke.'

'I need to go to the Kiev to win money.'

'Give me your phone number and I'll let you know when it's all clear.'

He gave me a mobile number and I gave him my card. He looked at it uncertainly.

'Why did you give me this?'

'When you're a lawyer you might need me.'
'I hope not.'
'What's the Russian word for knife?'
'*Nozh.*'

30

It was messy and I wasn't happy. Balakin was still around, presumably in the Bondi area, and not hiding. His appearance had changed enough to make him feel safe from the police, who didn't know his real identity and background anyway. The spooks did but, according to Josh, they were slow to organise themselves. I was best positioned to get him but that position wasn't secure. The waiter might tip Balakin off about me and so might Goldman, who I'd trust about as much as I would a horoscope.

Staking out the Kiev Café looked to be my best strategy but it wouldn't be easy and might not yield quick results. I drove home considering the options. Neville Kim had promised help. That could be useful for the stakeout but it meant losing control. Kim was vengeful and I knew nothing about the attitudes of his minions. The more I thought about it the messier it looked.

The house felt emptier than usual. They say that when you can't sleep you want to eat, a metabolic thing. I couldn't sleep and I didn't want to eat. I wanted to drink but I didn't. I thought of Pen and wondered how she was coping with her problems as I sat up, waiting for the dawn.

Of course I did fall asleep, somewhere around 5 am. The phone woke me a few hours later.

'Hardy,' I grunted.

'This is Sean Bright or whatever you might want to call me.'

I came instantly awake. 'I'd call you Stefan Balakin.'

'That'll do for now. You've already caused me a lot of trouble. My message to you is, back off.'

'So you can murder more women?'

'If I choose to, or maybe your daughter and your grandson. I know where they live.'

'They won't be there ten seconds after you hang up.'

'But I'm right outside and she's taking him to the crèche. Nice-looking boy, and she's cute.'

I was chilled and said nothing.

'Relax,' he said, 'I'm nowhere near Newtown. But you get the point. Back the fuck off!'

The line went dead. I sat listening to the hum and the thumping of my heart. I rang Megan.

'Where are you?'

'Home.'

'Good. Where's Ben?'

'In bed sick.'

'Good.'

'Good?' she said. '*Good*?'

I rang off. Thinking started a few seconds after that relief. *It had to be the waiter.*

Minutes later I was in the car, frowsy, unshaven, with dry, sore eyes and a leg threatening to cramp from the awkward position it had been in while I slept in the chair. I could taste the sourness of my breath. The early morning traffic was heavy; it seemed that every parent in Sydney was taking kids to school in badly driven SUVs.

I parked illegally outside the café. The bottle shop wasn't open at that hour but the patisserie was trading. I almost knocked down a man carrying his pastries away as I ran from the car into the café entrance. I pounded on the door with my fist. I kept pounding and was aware of people in the street making alarmed noises. The door opened and the fat waiter stood there in his pyjamas. I took a fistful of his pyjama jacket, rammed it into his second chin, and shoved him inside. I kicked the door shut and pushed him, stumbling, up the stairs.

Some lights were on in the café and I heaved him down into a chair. I stood over him. I was breathing hard, barely under control.

'Stefan Balakin,' I said. 'You know him. You've spoken to him. Where is he?'

His eyes rolled and blinked as he spluttered in Russian. I swatted him hard with an open hand.

'English!'

A voice came from the spiral staircase which presumably led to the living area. 'No need for that, Hardy. I'm right here. I thought you might come running.'

Balakin moved into a pool of light at the bottom of the staircase. Ten kilos lighter and with his hair cropped short, he was only barely recognisable as Sean Bright. He wore a white T-shirt and jeans. A sheathed knife was strapped to his right forearm and in his left hand he held a short-barrelled pistol.

31

A short-barrelled pistol has no range and poor accuracy, but that wasn't even in my thoughts as I launched a chair at Balakin almost before he'd finished speaking. I followed it, charging at him like a battering ram. The pistol fired twice and I felt heat and sensed something buzzing past me but all my energy was going into crushing Balakin. He'd threatened the two people I cared most about in the world and his little gun was no defence against my anger.

He slammed back against the bar; a stack of glasses crashed to the floor and the pistol flew across the room as he groped for support. I came in low and hooked him in the ribs trying to get his head down so I could use my fist to wreck his jaw and neck. It didn't work; he had a layer of muscle where my punch landed and the blow hurt me more than him.

The knife was in his hand now and he slashed, laying open the sleeve of my jacket from shoulder to wrist and slicing into my forearm. I scarcely felt the pain as I chopped at the hand holding the knife. He grunted as I connected but he kept his grip and brought the knife down again. It missed my face by a fraction. His knife hand was below waist level now and I grabbed it with both hands and drove it down. The knife dug into his thigh and he screamed as blood spurted like a fountain.

He stumbled sideways, knocking over two chairs and plucking at the knife with shaking hands. It fell free with a new gush of blood. I went after him again and drove a hard right into his sternum. I felt the bone break as he lurched backwards and fell down the stairs. He lay at the bottom near the door, crumpled like a crash-test dummy. He didn't move.

With blood running from my arm I went down the stairs and examined him. The angle of his head told the story. His neck was broken and he was dead. The blood from his leg wound had stopped spurting.

I went back to the café and found the waiter slumped in his chair. One of the bullets had hit him in the shoulder. He was covered in blood but it was Balakin's blood, not his own. He was in shock, staring at me and opening and closing his mouth with no sound coming out.

I worked my arms out of my jacket and let it fall to the floor. The cut on my forearm was long but not very deep. Blood was seeping out but not flowing. I went to the bar, grabbed a handful of paper napkins and used them to staunch the blood.

The waiter watched me and when it dawned on him that I wasn't going to hurt him he held out his hand. I gave him a wad of napkins and he pressed them to his shoulder.

'My nephew,' he said.

I nodded. My pulse was slowing, the adrenalin was draining away and I was starting to think. The room was a shambles with overturned chairs, blood everywhere, two wounded men and one dead. A bloodstained knife and a pistol lay on the floor and there was a bullet hole in a wall somewhere. Glass crunched under my feet with every step. Hard to explain and probably impossible to excuse.

I took out my mobile phone. The first thing I did was go halfway down the stairs and take a photograph of Balakin. It was difficult; my right hand throbbed and I could feel the internal damage. I had to use my left. Then I dialled a number.

'Josh,' I said. 'It's Hardy. I need some help.'

A clean-up team arrived ninety minutes later with Josh himself in command. By this time the waiter, who was actually the owner of the café, had had three vodkas and was feeling no pain. He said Balakin, who he knew by quite a different name, had been a thorn in his side for years. He'd told him about me and Balakin had orchestrated things from that point on.

'A bad man,' he said.

He didn't know how bad. I said, 'But a good chess player?'

'Not so good. People were afraid of him.'

'Not anymore,' I said.

He said something in Russian that sounded profound.

The team included a doctor who made arrangements for the bullet wound to be treated without being reported. The doctor cleaned and stitched my arm and gave me a tetanus shot and an antibiotic injection.

'Take it easy for a few days,' he said.

Josh said, 'He will.'

They fitted Balakin into a body bag and took him away, who knows where. Then they set about cleaning the café of any signs of disturbance. A .32 bullet was prised out of a wall and the hole filled; the glass was swept up, the floor was swabbed and surfaces were wiped. Josh talked intently to the café owner in Russian, drawing from him nods and what looked like pledges to cooperate.

'Your people are good,' I said to Josh.

'They are, but they're actually contractors.'

Jones was right, I thought.

It all took hours and I sat there answering questions from Josh. My arm ached and my hand had swollen to nearly twice its normal size. The doctor had examined it roughly and said it was bruised and tendons had been stressed but no bones were broken. Before he left I asked him what had killed Balakin.

He was a hard-eyed type with acne scars and tobacco breath, which he'd unsuccessfully tried to disguise with mints.

'You did,' he said. 'Either by severing an artery in his leg with the knife or by pushing him down the stairs. Take your pick.'

'He was holding the knife himself,' I said, 'and he fell.'

'That's your story.'

'That's enough,' Josh snapped. 'I saw your car outside. I'll have someone drive you home.'

'You'll have to find out where he lived and—'

'He didn't exist,' Josh said.

One of the clean-up guys had put my slashed jacket in a plastic bag. I had the sleeve of my shirt rolled almost to the shoulder and a gauze bandage covered my arm from the elbow to the wrist. I nodded my appreciation to the team and thanked Josh.

'You saved us a lot of trouble, Cliff,' he said. 'You gave us a silent kill.'

32

The rest of the day was a blur induced by the two injections, fatigue and the lousy feeling that comes from dropping down from a high adrenalin level. I slept, but not well; I drank more and ate less than I should have and slid into a low-blood-sugar torpor.

I cleaned myself up and regrouped the next day. I phoned Neville Kim and told him I had good news. He invited me to join him for lunch in a Korean restaurant in Surry Hills. We sat at a table for two where we received smooth, efficient service above the ordinary. When I commented on this he smiled.

'I have a substantial interest in the place. Now tell me your good news, Mr Hardy. I'm afraid I have to say you look somewhat strained, and I see your arm is bandaged.'

A spicy soup arrived. He'd ordered barbecued pork to follow and we were drinking OB beer. I traced the course of the investigation for him in detail.

'You should have asked for my help when you had narrowed your search down.'

'I thought about it, but events moved too quickly.'

I showed him the photograph on my phone of Balakin lying dead at the foot of the stairs. He looked at it for a long time.

'I would have preferred him to suffer in prison for twenty years, but I suppose that couldn't have been guaranteed.'

I shook my head. 'Nothing can be guaranteed.'

'That is true. I can tell people in my family that I'm satisfied Melanie has been avenged, even though I can't give them the details.'

'That's right, no details.'

'You did very well. I hope you've drawn all the appropriate fees and expenses.'

'I haven't thought about it but I will. Just keep the account open for a few days.'

'Of course. And what of the woman who helped you at various points?'

'She's gone.'

'I'm sorry.'

My arm healed. The police file on Sean Bright would remain open and Mrs Drake and the other connections of the girls killed would never receive closure. Timothy Polkinghorn was re-endorsed as a Liberal candidate and is mentioned as a likely Cabinet Minister if things go right for his party at the next election. In recent photographs he wears a pained expression as well he might, because 'Jones' and whoever he represents must have him by the balls.

Jack Buchanan bounced back and is doing well in sports production. Kelly Scott, looking and sounding like Marianne Faithfull, is trying to make a career as a singer. Rory O'Hara founded a radically green, radically anti-American party with a utopian agenda. After an initial flurry, its noise, in the run-up to the election, has died away to a whisper. From time to time I sniff the wind, surf the web and trawl the newspapers, and so far I've found no trace of Penelope Marinos. But I have a feeling I'll meet up with her again.